MAD CITY BUST

J.L. FREDRICK

To Roger & Kathy—
Enjoy!

"Joel"

1-25-2019

First Edition

ISBN: 0615746993
ISBN-13: 978-0615746999

Printed in the United States of America

For Scott

MAD CITY BUST

Chapter 1

Dear Michael,

> I could use that favor you think you owe me. If you can't make it as scheduled, change the reservation to suit you. But the sooner the better.

> As always, Donovan.

Mike Barnes had always known that someday he would have to pay off the debt he owed to Donovan Harlow. Knowing Harlow, it didn't seem particularly strange that a reminder of his obligation incurred in the Iraqi dessert should come years later. The method of approach, however, in its brevity and lack of explanation was a bit curious.

Mike read the letter several times over, trying to detect some hidden message. Then his eyes wandered to the airline tickets with his name printed on them, also included in the overnight *FedEx* envelope. He was to depart from J.F.K. on Monday afternoon; the return ticket had him leaving Madison, Wisconsin Friday night, arriving back in New York Saturday morning.

His grin spread a little wider as he leaned back in his

chair. He gazed out the window at concrete, steel, and reflective glass. It occurred to him that he had hardly been outside the city during the two years while he occupied a small office at Jackson & Grant business law firm.

From the back of his mind, a subconscious thought drifted to the forefront that any such request from Donovan Harlow could eventually involve trouble. Donovan Harlow, as he remembered him, had an affinity for trouble in various degrees. But for now, Mike thought he should avoid the negatives and focus on the benefits such a trip might bestow. One more glance out the window at the gray haze that hung bleakly among the rooftops convinced him that he was now anticipating the journey with great joy.

He was still feeling the lingering affects of a summer cold – not so severe that it kept him from working – but enough to weaken his performance. On Thursday, Mr. Jackson summoned him to his office on a routine matter, and when he noticed Mike still a bit sluggish, he suggested that a little vacation time might do some good. "Take a week off... get some fresh air. A Florida beach... or maybe the mountains in Colorado. Breathe some country air."

Mike babbled some words of appreciation and Jackson waved a gesture of approval. "I'll take care of it," he said. "Just let me know when you intend to leave."

A bit dazed by the good fortune, Mike returned to his office, consulted his checking account ledger, and calculated his available funds against the possible expenditures. When it appeared that a week of meals and lodging away from home seemed quite feasible, he picked up the phone to call Mr. Jackson's secretary with his planned days of absence.

The flight to Chicago went smooth and uneventful. After

he had gazed for a while at the shimmering waters of the Great Lakes passing thirty thousand feet below, he leaned back in the seat, closed his eyes, and tried to imagine why Donovan Harlow, after all these years, was requesting a favor. They had stayed in contact only on occasion. Since their year together in the Middle East, Mike had completed his law degree and landed a good job in New York. Donovan – well, Mike couldn't be sure of his exact profession, as Donovan was involved in several entrepreneurial endeavors. "He must've found trouble," was Mike's last thoughts. He awoke to a gentle hand on his shoulder, a stewardess informing him they would be landing in Chicago in about fifteen minutes.

Just then the pilot announced over the intercom that the weather in Chicago was sunny and clear, a balmy seventy-five degrees. It really didn't matter to Mike what the weather was – he didn't intend to breathe Chicago air.

For the two hour layover, he remained in the air conditioned O'Hare terminal, found a sandwich and a beer, a magazine and the most current edition of the Chicago Tribune.

Mike was a bit confused with the geography as the plane made its approach to the Dane County Airport at Madison. But then, although he'd never been there before, he remembered seeing on the map the large lakes around which the city was built, and the State Capital located on a narrow isthmus between the two largest. The spectacle of lights surrounding the lakes fell away as the wing dipped slightly and the plane banked toward the landing strip. As they angled down, he guessed that they were landing just north of the city. The captain had announced a little while before that the temperature at Madison was a pleasant sixty-eight degrees.

From the baggage claim area he headed directly to the main entrance. This was the air he wanted to breathe. A warm breeze caressed his nostrils as he stepped out onto the sidewalk and watched the passengers who had disembarked the flight with him. An Army Sergeant, apparently arriving home on leave, was met and hugged by a middle-aged couple. Mike assumed that they must be the young soldier's parents. Another older couple was affectionately greeted by some relative or friend and escorted to a waiting car. As Mike stood there considering the several taxis lined up at the curb, a tall, lanky, handsomely-dressed gentleman sidled up to him. "You must be Michael Barnes," he said with a half smile.

Mike was taken a little by surprise that anyone here would know him, but he nodded.

"Mr. Harlow sent me," the man said. "I'm here to drive you to your hotel."

Still somewhat dazed, Mike replied: "Very well, but which hotel would you recommend? I've never been to Madison."

"Oh! Mr. Harlow didn't inform you? Reservations have already been made for you at the Marriott."

Pleasantly surprised that he would not have to risk the possibility of poor accommodations at some low class motel, he nodded his approval as the man wrestled away his suitcase and gestured with his free hand to a highly polished black Lincoln Town Car at the curb. "Right this way," he instructed politely, put the suitcase in the trunk and opened the rear passenger door.

It was about a half-hour ride to the hotel, first northward out of the city sprawl adjacent the airport, and then west along a dark two lane highway, nearly deserted at almost midnight. After a few hills and curves, the lights of suburbia once again brightened the way, and Mike caught a brief glimpse of moonlight on water to his left, obviously one of the lakes he had seen from the air. He noticed a mix of quite old-looking houses and very modern business structures and apartment complexes, and it seemed rather appropriate on this street named Century Avenue.

A short time after the driver had turned onto an expressway, Mike spotted the bright red neon Marriott sign atop the tall hotel. Even in darkness, the area seemed a recent addition to the city; everything appeared new – even the street pavement looked as though it had not been there long.

The black sedan advanced slowly up the long driveway that dissected the giant parking area, and approached the main entrance under a great canopy on a side of the building that didn't face any street. Mike followed his driver through the revolving doors amidst a wall of glass. They approached the front desk where the driver set Mike's bag on the floor. Mike handed him a ten-dollar tip. The driver nodded, said "Thank you," and left.

A smartly-dressed clerk, equally as tall as Mike's driver, but with a scalp shaved smooth, emerged from a room behind the counter. He smiled cordially and asked if he could be of assistance.

"Is there a reservation for Barnes?"

The clerk scanned a couple of pages in a book. "Yes, Mr. Barnes," and produced a registration form and pen. "It appears that your accommodations for the week have been paid in advance," he said as he checked Mike's entries on the page.

Mike laid the pen on the counter, again, a little astonished. "Excuse me?"

"Yes... a Mr. Donovan Harlow has paid for your room.

Now, will you need any help with your baggage? I can call a bellman." He handed Mike an envelope.

Mike briefly studied the envelope with his name hand-written across the front. "No," he said. "I'll be fine."

"Very well," the clerk said as he handed Mike a key. "Room 601... sixth floor, straight ahead as you leave the elevator."

Mike peered into the night through the window of room 601. To the left were car lights streaking along the expressway. To the right he could see lights of the city, and beyond were pinpoints of red light marking a warning to aircraft of some tall towers.

He unpacked his suitcase, arranged his clothing in bureau drawers, hung his shirts, and sat on the edge of the king-sized bed. He had thought briefly of returning to the main floor, finding the lounge, and having a drink. But the more he contemplated, he realized he needed sleep more than a drink. Then he remembered the envelope the desk clerk had given him. He pulled it from his pocket, studied the hand-written name again, and then ripped it open. The signature – Donovan – was as he expected. But once again, the short message left him with questions. It read:

> Michael – Will call you in the morning. If anyone asks, you're here as a tourist.
>
> Donovan

Mike let out a groan that was part disappointment, but mostly irritation. He stuffed the folded paper back into the envelope, tossed it on the nightstand, undressed and stretched out on the cool sheets.

Chapter 2

The shrill ring of the telephone on the nightstand brought Mike abruptly out of a sound sleep at eight o'clock the next morning. He rolled over and grabbed for it with an automatic reaction, as if he were intent on silencing an alarm clock.

"Yeah?" he said, still groggy from sleep.

"Good morning, Sergeant. Did I wake you?"

The voice was not familiar after all these years, but the direct phrasing was. Mike Barnes was wide awake.

"Donovan?"

"Right. Have a good trip?"

"Yes, it was fine."

"Room okay?"

"It's great."

"Anything you want there, just sign the tab. This trip's on me, Kiddo. I'm damned glad you could make it. You get my note?"

"Yeah, sure. I'm a tourist."

Harlow laughed and then he was completely silent. When the silence became extended, Mike cleared his throat. "So... when do we get together?"

"Well..." Harlow hesitated. "It's like this. I have to go out of town today. I thought this might be a good time for you to do some sightseeing."

"Oh?"

"It's a nice day. You can get a rental car delivered right to the hotel. Check out the fair city of Madison. Our Capitol is pretty impressive, and there's the lakes, and you should take in Monona Terrace Convention Center... it was designed by

Frank Lloyd Wright, you know. There are a few good museums – seems to me I remember you as a history buff. And if you're into nature, there's the Arboretum, and then you can take a drive up Highway 12 to the Wisconsin River at Sauk City and watch for bald eagles."

Mike listened with part of his mind while a curious sort of annoyance edged its way into his thoughts. When he considered the curious notes and the hurried flight, the reminder of an old unpaid debt, the vague but exciting expectations of new adventure, he felt a little let down by all the talk of sightseeing.

"Thanks," he said.

"For what?"

"For planning my trip," Mike added with a little sarcasm. "I thought I came here to do you a favor."

"You will... I hope."

"Is there trouble?"

"For me, maybe. Not for you, though. Your part's legitimate. So quit worrying, okay? We can have dinner at my place. It's called Royal Palace, on State Street. Anyone can tell you where to find it."

"Royal Palace? What—"

"The best restaurant in town."

"Okay," Mike uttered, finding it difficult to associate the best restaurant in town with the man he had known as Lieutenant Harlow. "I didn't know you ran a restaurant."

"I don't," Harlow responded. "I just own it. Seven thirty okay with you?"

"Whatever you say, Lieutenant."

"Seven thirty, then. And remember... you're still just a tourist."

For the lack of anything better to do, Mike called for a rental car to take advantage of this time to see what Madison had to offer. Although Harlow had offered to pay all expenses, Mike thought he would use his own credit card for the car to avoid confusion. While he waited for its delivery, he picked up a few visitor brochures and a city map from the gift shop, found a comfortable couch in the main atrium, and tentatively planned an itinerary for the day.

The dark blue Mercury sedan proved to be a comfortable car, and the day couldn't have been any better to casually enjoy the sights of an unfamiliar town. Mike tried to remember all the tips Donovan had given him, and when he had walked around the Capital Square, toured Monona Terrace, and lounged in a city park by the lake with his fast food lunch, he found his way back to Highway 12 and headed north. He didn't see many eagles at the river, but it was an enjoyable ride through the country, and he was grateful to spend some time in the fresh air. His summer cold was already fading.

It was after five o'clock when Mike Barnes returned to his hotel room. He had taken off his shirt, getting ready for a shower, when he remembered a couple of calls he was to make, sat down with the phone book, and looked up the numbers. The first call was to an acquaintance he had gone to school with, John Findley, who had accepted a job offer with a Madison firm. When they had brought each other up to date on matters of mutual interest, they agreed to get together the next evening for a couple of drinks. The second call was to a newspaper, the *State Journal*. A colleague in the New York office had given him the name of a friend, Scott Newman, who worked at the paper, and it wouldn't hurt to make a new acquaintance in the news media. But when the receptionist said Scott had already left, he made a mental note to try again the next day.

State Street seemed as busy at seven-thirty in the evening as it had during the day. Once the blocks of student tenements – some shabby, and some elegant – gave way to the business section, the lights were bright, the sidewalks crowded, and the hum of traffic endless. It reminded him of a subdued version of New York, without the jungle of skyscrapers. A police car was parked on the corner, and beyond, music spilled out from the open doors of a popular night spot. Taxis stood at the curb, the drivers alert for a potential fare. This was supposed to be the "off season" for college students, but the area was still quite lively. Mike thought he surely couldn't be the only "tourist" out on the town that night.

Another block down the street, Mike stopped in front of a small but colorful neon sign that read: *The Royal Palace.* Luck was with him, as he found a parking space just around the corner.

Beneath the sign Mike stepped through a dimly lit foyer into a long, narrow room, soft but adequate lighting, high ceilings, and the royally elegant theme of a castle. At the left were a series of booths along the wall, with tables at the center, all dressed in royal purple coverings. A string quartet played softly in the far corner by a baby grand piano, and to one side of the service door, stairs flanked by wrought iron railings led to a small balcony and a single door.

To Mike's immediate right was a semi-circular bar. Donovan Harlow sat on one of the stools, a drink in front of him. He saw Mike almost at once and came to greet him with outstretched hand. "Hiya, Kiddo," he said beaming a toothy grin.

"Hello, Donovan."

They stood there a long moment inspecting each other, aged, now, from when they had last been together, Harlow four or five years older and a couple of inches shorter than Barnes, but still with that air of dignified arrogance that had always irritated Mike.

It had been about ten years since Mike last saw Harlow while he was in law school. Donavan had dropped in and bunked for a few days in his apartment. Except for the healthy-looking tan, a few wrinkles at the corners of his eyes, and perhaps a few added pounds, he could see little change in the man, and he told him so.

"Same with you, Kiddo," Harlow said. "Except maybe you look a little soft."

"That's what office work does to a person."

"Well, you can have it. Personally, I like the outdoors... Sit down, Michael. What would you like to drink?"

"If the bartender can make a good one, an Old Fashioned."

"He can... Perry," he called to the barman. "A special Old Fashioned for my friend." He finished his drink and pushed the highball glass across the bar. "And another *Seagram's* and water for me." Giving his attention to Mike again, he said: "How'd it go today? Buy any good souvenirs?"

"Some."

"For your girlfriends?"

"For my sister and my secretary."

"What? No lady friends? What the hell's the matter with you?" Harlow turned to intercept a stocky, dark skinned man, middle-aged, neatly trimmed mustache shadowing a pleasant smile. Immaculate in a pale blue tuxedo, he held a menu under his arm, and when Harlow made the introduction he bowed from the waist in a stiff, sophisticated manner.

13

"An old friend," Harlow said. "Michael Barnes – Eduardo Espinosa. Eduardo is probably the best maitre de this side of Saint Thomas. Right, Eduardo?"

Espinosa smiled cordially. "If you say so, senór."

"We would like a table in about twenty minutes," Harlow said.

When Eduardo had withdrawn, Donovan leaned toward Mike. "Without Eduardo this would be just another eating place." Then, in his unusual manner he refocused on Mike. "Well," he said. "How's the law business?"

They had another drink and fifteen minutes of casual conversation, all of it unimportant, none of it touching on why Mike was here under somewhat unusual circumstances. When Eduardo came to announce the table was ready, Harlow guided Mike toward the woman sitting at the end of the bar.

She was a made-over blonde of twenty-five or so. Her long eye lashes were thick with mascara, and she wore a low-cut evening dress, nicely bulging. Her brown eyes looked tired, and the corners of her painted lips drooped until she gave a token smile.

"Bridget Palmer," Donovan said. "She'll sing for us later. This is Michael Barnes, visiting from New York for a few days," he said to the girl. He turned to Mike again. "Bridget was an activity director at a resort. They gave her the boot, so I persuaded her to move in here and entertain the customers with her songs. Plays a nice piano, too."

"Just chords, mostly," the girl admitted. "It isn't much."

"Stop by for a brandy," Harlow said, and then he led Mike to the booth that was set and waiting.

The steak Harlow had ordered was tender and expertly broiled. The Delmonico potatoes, perfect, with just the right amount of cheese. When Espinosa stopped by to see if everything was all right, Mike complimented the establishment and praised the chef.

"I ordered steak," Harlow said, "just to show you we could do it as well as anyplace in New York. And tomorrow, you should try our fried shrimp. I think you'll find them as good as any you've ever eaten. Right, Eduardo?"

The maitre de just smiled, bowed, and went away. Harlow leaned back and gazed about the room with approval of all the diners occupying every table. He asked again about the tour Mike had made of the city, wanting details, and every now and then throwing in bits of local color. It seemed to Mike that he was deliberately avoiding any mention of the purpose for the hurried trip and the mysterious note that started it all.

At first, Mike had put aside his curiosity, and had tried to keep speculations to a minimum. Apparently, Harlow enjoyed playing the host and wanted to make him feel welcomed. But now he had decided there must be some other reason for this peculiar treatment causing him discomfort and frustration. Harlow was stalling. So what? Mike asked himself. Harlow was picking up the tab, wasn't he? If he wanted to postpone his request for the favor – whatever that might be – what difference did it make?

This line of reasoning did little to ease Mike's anxiety, and when Donovan asked Bridget Palmer to join them for a drink, Mike leaned back, sulking, determined that he would refrain from asking any further questions until Harlow was ready to hear them.

Bridget's presence did little to disperse his mood. She gave him a fleeting smile when she sat down, but there was discontent in her gaze, and she made no comment when Harlow told her how he and Mike had fought the war in

Kuwait. It was mostly monologue and it continued until a waiter stopped by, leaned close to Donovan, and whispered some words in Spanish.

Harlow glanced toward the bar and stood up. Excusing himself, he zigzagged through the tables to the bar and two men standing there. Both were dark-complected, one of average height and stocky, the other a little taller and wearing dark glasses. All three went into a huddle. Mike glanced at the girl. She was still watching Donovan, her expression drooping between sips of her drink, and oblivious of Mike's stare. He was much aware that she had a very shapely figure, although, perhaps a little plump, nice hands and well-kept nails. He watched her watching Donovan for a minute or two. "How long were you at the resort?" he said when he grew tired of her neglect.

"What?" Her glance came around quickly. Just for a moment, her heavily shadowed eyes appeared embarrassed. "I guess I was daydreaming."

"You were a long way off."

"Not so far," she said, staring at her drink.

"I just asked how long you were at the resort."

"Eleven months."

"Did you sing there, too?"

"No... well... once in a while the band would let me sing a chorus of something and maybe shake a tambourine."

"Didn't you like it?"

"Being an entertainment director?" She shrugged her bare shoulders. "It was okay, but I thought I'd rather *be the entertainment*... a singer." She made a disgusted little grunt. "How crazy is that?" she said and looked away.

Mike glanced around to see Harlow still talking with the two men, and now he wondered if the ex-lieutenant of Delta

Company could be the reason for Bridget's discontent.

A waiter came by with a tray, replaced their empty glasses with fresh drinks, and promptly went away. Bridget finished hers quickly and stood. She said it was time for a song. Mike saw that the string quartet had packed their instruments, and the stage was empty and dark.

Bridget strolled to the piano, turned on a light, adjusted the microphone, and then hit some rather lazy chords, moving not too skillfully into an introduction. She sang a Jimmy Buffet tune, and by that time, Mike knew she was right when she said she only played chords. Her voice was pleasant enough in a husky sort of way for a woman, but her range seemed limited, and the performance lacked professional glow. She'd never make it on American Idol, but here it sounded okay and the diners rewarded her with modest applause.

During her third song, Mike watched Donovan leave the pair at the bar. He pulled a chair up to a table occupied by two middle-aged couples, the women dressed rather classy, and the men in casual suits and open-necked shirts. Mike Barnes made no attempt to keep track of time, but as he watched Harlow move from table to table, his good nature started to withdraw. The drinks didn't help, and more than once he was tempted to get up and just leave. But that wouldn't bring him to any resolution. He decided to wait for Harlow, and then he would ask pointblank just what he wanted.

It was after eleven and the place half empty when Donovan eventually came to the booth and sat down. The waiter brought him a drink. He tasted it, and wiped the perspiration from his brow. "Every night I have to pamper the customers. They spend a lot here, but they're sensitive... they expect a little personal attention. How you doin'? Okay?

Enough to drink?"

"Plenty," Mike responded. "You sure you can spare the time?"

Harlow's eyes widened as he recognized the overtones of resentment in Mike's response. He grinned. "You're sore, I guess, eh?"

"Just a little. I get that crazy letter and airline tickets from you. It was only dumb luck that I had an opportunity to get away from the office on such short notice. I get out here on *your* schedule, because I owe you something and I want to pay off. So what happens? You're out of town. You stall. You won't talk."

"Relax, Kiddo." Donovan patted Mike's elbow. "I did have to go out of town, to Milwaukee to see a guy. You're only here for a few days, so I thought you'd want to see the sights. I planned on showing you the town tonight, but it turns out I can't." His smile faded and his gaze became distant. "I'm in a bit of a jam. I guess you figured that out."

Mike sat back, expecting to finally hear Donovan's request.

"I'm gambling that you will help me if you can," Donovan went on. "But I have to talk to you – alone – somewhere where it's quiet. I have to explain something I doubt you'd know about and..."

The rest of his thought was left unsaid. Mike saw his gaze focus beyond the booth; Donovan's eyes widened and his jaw dropped. Mike tried to contain his obvious surprise, turned, and was nearly face-to-face with a big blond-haired man in a well worn leather jacket. A big grin spread across the man's soft-looking face. "Surprised?" he said as he reached for Harlow's glass.

"What happened, Abe?" Donovan said quietly.

The big man took a gulp from the glass and set it down. "I got a ride," he said, and with no more than a glance at Mike, he headed for the bar.

Harlow watched him as he stopped beside the piano and caressed Bridget's shoulder with his hand. She responded with a wink and a funny little loving sort of smile. Harlow stood, still watching the man he called Abe. Over his shoulder he said to Mike, "Tomorrow, Kiddo. Tomorrow for sure. If you want to look around, there's plenty of places in Mad City."

When Donovan started for the bar, Mike slid out of the booth and headed toward the entrance without glancing back, just a little angry, but mostly frustrated in spite of his efforts to show his disappointment. He walked along the sidewalk, viewing the many bright signs and inviting places. A few short years ago when he was still a college boy, he would have jumped at this opportunity. But it occurred to him that he had already had enough to drink and he was in no mood for this sort of entertainment. Turning abruptly, he went directly to his rented car and jerked open the door.

Chapter 3

Mike Barnes was awake early the next morning, and without even looking to see the time, he rolled over and attempted to sleep a while longer. But the ringing telephone brought him back to consciousness, and he didn't have to wonder who might be on the other end.

"How'd you do last night?" Harlow's unmistakable voice asked.

"Did okay. Came back to the hotel and went to bed."

"Smart, Kiddo. How about three o'clock this afternoon?"

"Fine with me, Lieutenant."

"At my place, then."

"The restaurant?"

"No. My apartment. It's at the back of the restaurant building, but the front entrance is on the block behind the Palace." He gave the address. "The office in the restaurant connects with the one in my apartment, but you'd better come the other way. I'll be expecting you."

Mike decided he'd take full advantage of Harlow's hospitality after he hung up the phone. He called for room service to deliver breakfast – Belgian waffles with fresh strawberries, papaya juice and coffee. When the order came, he drew the drapes fully open, flooding the room with glorious sunshine. The food, the view, and the bright, cloudless morning served to erase the gloom that had infected him the night before. It occurred to him that he only had a couple more days here, and he was determined to enjoy them. After he shaved and showered, he put on shorts and a Hawaiian shirt, and headed down to the main floor atrium with the copy of *USA Today* that had been dropped at his door sometime during the wee hours. When he had had his fill of news, he went to the pool for a swim, and when lunchtime rolled around, he had a sandwich and a beer in the hotel's Tiffany Grille Restaurant.

Mike Barnes was in an exceptionally good mood by two-thirty when he sauntered into the *State Journal* offices and asked for Scott Newman. Upon hearing his request, a young woman behind the counter walked to a group of people huddled together around a small table. The man who stood up and followed her looked to be in his late thirties, casually dressed in khakis and sport shirt, a pencil tucked behind his ear where the hair had started to turn gray.

"I'm Scott Newman," he offered.

"Mike Barnes. Andy Johnson told me to look you up... said you were stationed in Germany with him."

"Andy Johnson? Sure. How do you know Andy?"

"We work in the same office in New York. I thought maybe we could get together for dinner or drinks..." Mike glanced around the room, noticing the activity. "Is this an afternoon paper? Did I come at a bad time?"

"The *Capital Times* is, but it's already at press. We're just brainstorming for tomorrow's headlines." Newman reached for a scratch pad on the counter and wrote a number. "Here's my cell phone. You stayin' at a hotel?"

"The Marriott... I guess it's on the west side of town."

"Great. Give me a call this evening. I'll probably be at the *Paradise* with a brew in my fist."

"Paradise?"

"Yeah. It's a great bar and grill... out near your hotel. The desk clerk can tell you where it is."

Donovan Harlow's apartment was among a row of weathered and gray looking brick and stucco two-story buildings fronting a narrow street and not far from the corner. Only a ten-foot alley separated Harlow's building from its neighbor, and a sign tacked to a heavy wooden gate blocking the gap said: Private Property.

An electric lock buzzed just seconds after Mike pressed the doorbell. He entered into a foyer with stairs leading upward to a landing where a door opened and Donovan appeared.

The apartment was more than Mike had expected – comfortably elegant. The living room appeared much larger than it really was with cathedral ceiling, cream-colored walls contrasting sharply with the darker stained oak woodwork, and highly polished hardwood floor. The furniture was mostly dark-colored, masculine-looking, and plush. Only a few oil paintings –tropical scenes, mostly – graced the otherwise bare walls. An arched opening to one side gave way to a modern kitchen and dining room. To the rear, another doorway led into a large bedroom. After the heat of the city streets, the cool air was refreshing.

"Let's go in here," Donovan said as he led the way through the bedroom with its massive bed, fine oak bureau, and adjoining bath. He opened another door that led to his private office. As Mike followed, he took mental note of the iron grillwork protecting the bedroom windows. The posh continued in the office furnished with oak desk and cabinets, easy chairs and sofa. At the far end, a heavy metal door connected this room with the restaurant office.

Harlow directed Mike to a comfortable chair next to the desk, and then sat down behind his desk. He passed a humidor of cigars across the desk, and when Mike declined, Donovan took one out and lit it. He leaned back in his chair with a good-natured twist in his smile. "I guess you thought

22

you'd have to smuggle me out of the country or break me out of prison, eh, Kiddo?"

Mike shrugged his shoulders, remembering this man he had briefly known during the Gulf War. They had never been close friends, and they never could be. To Mike Barnes, Donovan Harlow possessed some unpleasant quality that greatly diminished the element of trust. But he had learned to accept that, just as he accepted the fact that he had an obligation to carry out. "What difference does it make? I'm here now," he said, matching Donovan's grin.

"Yeah," Harlow said. "I suppose it doesn't." His grin faded. "It's about my son. I thought of you because you're a lawyer, and you know how to handle things. And you're the one guy I know that's really honest."

Mike fought the urge to be astonished. He sat in silence, finding nothing to say. The ex-lieutenant was displaying a side of his character that Mike had never seen before.

Donovan settled back in his chair again. "Maybe you didn't know about my son," he went on. Distance grew in his gaze. "Or even that I was married. Well, it was a bad marriage, and I don't regret the divorce. But, the boy... I've been thinking about the boy. He'll be seven in a couple of months, and I want to do something for him." He refocused his gaze on Mike. "I suppose you think I'm acting a little late."

"What?"

"I mean, you're probably thinking why I waited so long to be a father to the boy." Donovan sighed. "Maybe the answer is that a guy like me has to reach a certain point when he wonders if he'll get to see the kid at all... before the kid figures out what the score is." Putting his cigar aside, he pulled open the top drawer, retrieved a check, stared at it a long moment, and then shoved it across the desk.

Mike examined it without touching it. It was made out in the amount of thirty thousand dollars to Michael Barnes, drawn on the Chase Manhattan Bank.

"For the kid's education," Harlow said. "College when he's ready for it. You handle this for me and we're square – not that you ever really owed me anything."

"And just how do you want me to *handle* it?"

"How should I know? That's your business. Maybe some secure investment... or annuity... or maybe a trust fund."

Mike listened to every word, but this was so unexpected, and so unlike his impression of Harlow's character, that he was slow to process the thought. "But... what about the boy's mother? Why can't you just give her— "

"Because the bitch won't have any part of me." Harlow grunted a few words of profanity. "When I first came here, I didn't' have any to send and—"

"You ran out on her?"

"Well, yeah. I told you it didn't work out." Harlow winced, and then went on with the original thought. "When things started coming around for me, I wrote and enclosed a check, but she sent it back. She didn't want my money or anything else from me... ever." In that moment his dark eyes turned cold, glaring out from beneath hard, black brows with a steely luster, the way Mike remembered them. "Well, I can do this if I want to, and she can't stop me."

"All right," Mike said, more believing now. "But why don't you go to New York and do this yourself?"

"Because I'm not so sure that I'd make it. There's some around here that would just as soon stick a knife in my back," Donovan said with more contempt than concern. "Sure, I've taken some shortcuts here and there. I've always played the odds. That's the way I operate. But there's hotheads in this world. You accidently step on some toes and... well... you know how it is. There's somebody who wants your blood." He paused a few moments, and then added matter-of-factly, "Somebody took a shot at me from an alley a few days ago."

Mike took it all in, silently attempting to glean from it the hidden reason for his involvement. He found nothing particularly startling in the statements he heard, considering the man who made them.

Donovan flicked the ashes and relit his cigar. "I have some business matters to handle in Minneapolis. If all goes well there, I'll probably come to New York, and then—"

As if to back up his statement, a knock from the steel door connecting the two offices interrupted him. When Harlow opened the door its angle blocked the visitor from Mike's view, but he easily heard the voice.

"You heard anything yet?" The man's voice seemed familiar, but Mike couldn't put a face with it right away.

"No," Donovan said bluntly. "I told you I'd let you know just as soon—"

"The stuff was delivered."

"Okay."

"So what's holding things up?"

"I talked to Delsoto a little while ago. He said he hasn't heard a thing."

"The word's goin' around," the unseen visitor said, "that you're leavin' town."

"If I do, you'll still have the Cessnas."

"That ain't the point. I want my cut and—"

"When I get it."

"Shit."

Harlow stood poised and ready, the cigar still between his fingers, his lips pressed tightly together. A gleam of perspiration began to show on his brow. He shifted his weight back away from the door. "If you need a few hundred bucks right now, you can have it," he said. "Otherwise, you'll wait... just like me."

The man had moved into the room while Harlow spoke. Mike recognized him, now, as the one who had come to the table the night before, and then moved on to chat with Bridget Palmer. Now, in better light, Abe's thick, wavy blond hair looked shaggy and in need of a trim, and his tan khakis and loud sport shirt were wrinkled. Added frustration came to his sullen expression as he noticed Mike, stared for a moment, and then looked back to Harlow. He was suddenly gone from view, but his voice trailed behind. "I'll be around. Either I get my cut, or you don't go anywhere."

Harlow closed the door and came back to his chair. "Pilot," he said. "We've been partners in a charter flight service. He still has some equity in a couple of Cessnas and an old DC-3."

Harlow relit his cigar and leaned back in his chair. As though there had been no interruption, he glanced at Mike. "So, what do you say, Kiddo? Can you do it?"

Mike already knew his answer. There had been time for his mind to turn back to that night in Kuwait, to understand for the hundredth time that if it were possible for one man to save another man's life twice in one day, Harlow had done just that.

During the bloodiest attack by the Iraqi Army on U.S. troops in convoy to liberate Kuwait, Donovan Harlow's initial effort was to pull Mike Barnes, badly wounded and unconscious, from an overturned and burning Hummer. Hours later, it had been the struggle to reach safety, and only Harlow could know how he had dragged and carried his unconscious burden there.

Michael Barnes had been a green sergeant of twenty at the time; Harlow a second lieutenant and combat experienced. Until the day in '95 when Harlow turned up in New York, Mike had seen him only briefly in the German hospital. Understanding what had happened, Mike had searched his soul to express his gratitude, but found little to say. All he could convey was a simple "Thanks."

Harlow had grinned. "Forget it," he had said. "It all evens out. Maybe you can do a favor for me someday."

But it had not been an easy matter to dismiss such an obligation. The memory of it would haunt Mike every now and then, and when Harlow had looked him up in New York, he had felt certain that a request was forthcoming. His concern, then, was that he would be able to fulfill his obligation, if asked. Instead, Harlow had just gone on his way, leaving behind a brief note thanking him for the use of his couch and that he would be in touch again soon. After that, there were occasional letters from various locations – Key West, the Bahamas, and even Panama – and each time he opened an envelope from Donovan, he anticipated a request and an end to this maddening mind game.

Perhaps the reason for his concern was just knowing the man. Although their association had not been long, Mike had known him as a craftsman in warfare and one who would never take a prisoner. He had a certain air of ruthlessness, and he defied anyone who got in his way.

But for a man who seemed to lack such things as compassion or respect for the rights of others, he was still a personable man, and under that skin-deep sort of charm, was a man of confidence, a gambler who always seemed to hold a winning hand. Maybe that was why Mike had felt an odd sense of relief when he received the note and the tickets. Although he suspected there might be trouble involved, he had been eager to come, because once the favor was completed, the haunting reminder of an obligation would be out of his mind forever. It had never occurred to him that there could be a flaw in Harlow's armor, and that made this particular request seem surprising and unexpected. But now that he understood how Harlow felt about his young son, he didn't hesitate.

"Of course, Donovan," he said. "I'll work something out. I don't know what, yet, but—"

"Whatever you work out is okay with me," Harlow interrupted. "I know you'll do right." He let out a sigh of relief, and then smiling as if being entertained, he pulled open a desk drawer. "There's a couple of things I'd like you to take back to New York for me. Do you remember Gordy Trapp?"

Mike shook his head. "Don't think so."

"Sure you do... the supply clerk from Long Island... well, maybe he went back to the States before you got there."

"Maybe," Mike said. He stared at the combination cigarette case and lighter Harlow had produced – an ugly imitation tortoise shell trinket that could only have been made as a tourist trap novelty. His expression must have reflected his opinion.

Donovan chuckled. "You wouldn't be caught dead with a thing like this... you're too Ivy League. But Gordy will love it. He's a souvenir hound." He spun the flint wheel, but without fuel it just sparked. Then he opened the case and removed the tissue paper, exposing the shiny metal interior. "Gordy doesn't have your education, but he's one I can trust, too. He knows about the boy, and he's been keeping an eye on things for me. I'll have him meet you at the airport, and he can fill you in."

Donovan slid open another drawer and then glanced at the table behind his chair. "There's a box for this," he said, tapping the cigarette case. "Maybe it's in the bedroom. Look on the bureau, will you, Kiddo?"

Mike went into the other room and almost immediately spotted the box. When he returned, Harlow was opening a much smaller box.

"I got this for the kid," he said. "How could his mother refuse to let him keep something like this? What do you think?"

Mike shook his head, a little moved by the sight of the gold St. Christopher medal and thin gold chain. Donovan's smile softened as he replaced the medal and the cigarette case in their respective boxes and secured the tops with rubber bands. "You probably shouldn't put these in any carry-on luggage – they'll set off the metal detector at the airport."

A bell rang somewhere close. Mike assumed it was the doorbell. Donovan quickly stood and moved through the bedroom. A few seconds later, Mike heard the front door open, and with it came the sound of a woman's voice. Donovan and his visitor remained in the living room, so Mike didn't hear their low-spoken conversation. Not more than two or three minutes later, the bell rang again, and the conversation in the living room fell into dead silence for a few seconds, followed by quick, light footsteps progressing toward the office.

Mike saw the woman first, and he stood as a respectful gesture. The strikingly attractive brunette in a pale yellow dress hesitated when she eyed him. She had an erect, haughty way of carrying herself that did nice things for her slim, shapely form. Impressed with her pretty face and almost regal appearance, Mike pegged her at thirty-something. A bit of astonishment was in her green eyes, yet in that moment he recognized a quality in her that might be worthwhile to any man who could attract and hold her affection. The moment passed and she glanced over her shoulder to Donovan.

"It's all right," he said. "An old Army buddy. Very discreet." He stepped past her, opened the door to the restaurant office, and took her arm guiding her through. When he closed it again, he immediately started for the living room. "This could be trouble," he said quietly. His expression hadn't changed.

When the front door opened, Mike heard a man's voice, but at first, the words were indistinct. He moved to a vantage point where he could see beyond the bedroom and into the living room, and then he could hear them talking, too.

"A man has a right to protect his house against thieves," the visitor said. "I think the same thing holds true with his wife."

Harlow moved slowly backward, his hands loose at his sides. The small gray-haired man who had just entered wore a light gray suit, one hand in the jacket pocket, and by the way the fabric extended gave Mike the impression that the hidden hand held a gun. He matched Harlow's slow movement toward the office with a high-shouldered, stiff-backed, deliberate step.

"You've got your signals crossed, Major," Harlow spoke quietly.

"Celeste has led me to believe otherwise. That's why I'm here. I'm telling you for the last time—" At that moment he spotted Mike and stopped short.

Harlow glanced over his shoulder. "Mr. Barnes," he said to the man, "will tell you that no one else has been here."

The major's grimaced expression swept across the bedroom, and for a few seconds, his eyes shot out flames of hatred, and Mike feared what might happen next. Then, as though his standards of conduct prevented anything further, he turned abruptly and stalked back through the living room. The door slammed and the room fell into total silence.

Beads of perspiration glistened on Harlow's forehead. He produced a muffled little growling sound in his throat as he stepped back into the office. When he finally spoke, his voice sounded relieved. "Thanks."

"For what?"

"For being here. The major had worked up quite a head of steam."

Mike shrugged. "He had a gun, too." He couldn't resist one more question. "I guess the woman who just breezed through a little while ago was Celeste?"

Donovan smiled.

"Nice."

"Yeah," Harlow said, but before he could continue, the phone rang. He picked it up on the first ring. The clipped replies revealed nothing: "Okay... Yeah... Good... Right away." As quickly as he had picked up the receiver, he slammed it down again. "Look," he said turning to Mike. "I have to go out. There's liquor in the cabinet in the living room, and plenty of ice in the fridge. Help yourself." He pointed to the two small boxes on the desk. "Just be sure to put these in your pocket before you leave."

Mike just stood there until the metal door clicked shut. He pocketed the souvenir boxes, went slowly into the living room, opened the cabinet doors and inspected the variety of bottles. The afternoon heat had started to filter into the apartment, and the thought of a cool drink was inviting, but after a moment of indecision he closed the cabinet doors. It was too early for a drink.

He was only four feet from the door when the doorbell sounded. The slender young woman who stood on the landing when he opened the door seemed strangely familiar. She wore a simple print sun dress and carried a straw handbag. Her long, bare legs, arms and face were nicely tanned, and her sandy-colored hair, sun-bleached. The fiery gleam in her eyes showed determination as she stepped past him through the open door and into the room.

"I'm Lori McKay," she announced, foregoing any preliminaries.

Mike grinned. He couldn't help it. It was a spontaneous reaction spurred by the sight of this girl – definitely a *ten!* "How do you do?" he said, which was promptly ignored.

"I've come for the twenty-five thousand dollars you owe my father," she said. "I have the note and his power of attorney."

Mike made no reply. At that moment, her words meant nothing to him, and he only felt an uncontrollable urge to know this girl. What appeared to be anger did not prevent Mike from seeing the girl of his dreams – the sort of girl he had always envisioned to meet someday, and now, understanding that she thought he was Donovan Harlow, a sense of exhilaration worked on him. "You're not from around here, are you?" he said.

"You know very well where I'm from," she responded coldly. "My father sent you four letters, and I've written you twice. And now I have a lawyer here in Madison."

"Well, you—"

"I thought I should come here first," she continued, ignoring the interruption. "There shouldn't be any need for a lawyer. It would be so much easier for us both if you would just simply pay what you rightfully owe my father."

Mike heard her out, paying little attention, inspecting her gorgeous green eyes and the curve of her cheeks. He smiled graciously and he knew it was time to end this mistaken identity.

"I'm Michael Barnes," he said. "Mr. Harlow just left a few minutes ago. He wasn't sure when he'd be back."

For the first time since she arrived, she actually looked at Mike's face, and it was then that she realized the dark-haired young man staring from five or six inches above her was rather handsome. As though she were evaluating his sincerity, she seemed to understand he spoke the truth. Embarrassment flooded her cheeks, and Mike thought it made her look even lovelier. She started to apologize in a small voice. "I'm sorry. I just assumed... I mean..."

"It's okay," Mike replied. Would you want to wait?"

"Oh, no... thank you, just the same." She shifted her handbag and drew back, smiling faintly. The confusion was still working on her, and her eyes evaded Mike as she reached for the door.

Not wanting her to leave so suddenly, Mike asked, "Are you staying at a hotel? Can I give you a lift?"

"I'm at the Marriott," she said. "And no, I have a cab waiting."

He followed her down the stairs to the foyer. A little inner excitement remained. She was staying at the Marriott, and somehow he knew he would see her again.

Chapter 4

I t was nearly five when Mike Barnes returned to the hotel. He went right to the front desk to inquire of Lori McKay's room number. Informed that it was 306, he was content with that for the time being. His sense of pride prevented him from making a direct call at her door so soon, but if he happened to see her in the atrium or the restaurant or the lounge, that would be another matter entirely. He checked the pool area first, and then strolled around the main atrium, past the Tiffany Grille, and to the cocktail lounge. A few men were seated at the bar in various attire – business suits to golf shirts. Several tables were occupied by men and women, and Mike, with cunning strategy selected a small table, taking a chair facing the atrium.

He slipped off his sport jacket, draped it over the back of the chair, and ordered an Old Fashioned, all the while keeping an eye on the entrance and the atrium. When the drink came, he reached into his jacket pocket for his cigarettes and a lighter. His fingers touched the boxes Donovan had given him. As the events of the day came back to him, he thought of the St. Christopher medal and Donovan's young son in New York. A little guilt and shame filtered into his feelings when he considered how wrong he had always been about Harlow, certain that he could not possibly feel compassion or sentiment. Now, with a little analyzing, he could understand his reasons for the past conclusion. Donovan had always been tough and strong-willed; his energy was never diverted by outside influences; rarely was he concerned about the opinions of others.

Donovan was in trouble now – it was evident simply by the statements he made and by the incidents Mike had already witnessed. But all that was Donovan's affair, Mike thought, not his. His assignment from Donovan had turned out to be quite simple, and it seemed to be legitimate. It was a relief just to have made it to that point, but as his thoughts moved on and he ordered another drink, he thought of Lori McKay again, and he wondered why Harlow owed her father twenty-five thousand dollars.

He was still wondering about it when he saw her – only a quick glimpse as she swung around the corner and headed toward the elevators. Leaving his jacket and unfinished drink he stumbled to his feet, and made a hasty attempt to intercept her. But he was too late; both elevator doors were closed when he reached them. He quickly pressed the button, waited impatiently until one car returned, and then rode to the third floor. On his way along the balcony to room 306, his mind raced in an effort to find the proper greeting when she opened the door.

But there was no answer, and Mike accepted the fact that she had not gone to her room. He hurried back to the elevators and once again pressed the button to summon a car. As he stepped inside the car that stopped he asked the couple if they had by chance seen her. "A slender, brown-haired girl got off on the eighth floor as we were getting on," they said.

Mike rode up to eight, less expectant, now, of seeing Lori. As he exited the elevator, he heard voices and laughing, and noticed an open door to the left. He slowly stepped closer, and then he saw her just inside the door, turned away from him, talking to the occupants of the room – a smartly-dressed middle-aged woman and a much younger man, perhaps about his own age. The woman noticed him, so he continued on down the balcony to the service stairs, accepting this temporary failure with no desire to barge in on strangers.

He went down the two flights to his floor, casually strolled to his room, mumbling bits of disappointment to himself as he pulled the key from his pocket and opened the door. As it closed behind him he wondered why he hadn't returned to the lounge for his jacket and drink, and at that moment he became aware that something was wrong in his room. His suitcase that he had left closed on the floor beside the bureau was now spread open on the bed. A bureau drawer was pulled out and some of his things were scattered on the top. Mike hesitated for a moment while he formulated the idea of leaving everything as it was, return to the lobby and request at the front desk that a report be made to security personnel. But before he could make his exit from the room, two men stepped out from around the corner of the bathroom. One of them held a short-barreled revolver pointed at Mike. They stared at each other for a few seconds, silent and motionless, and it was then that Mike knew he had seen these men before. They had been at the Royal Palace bar the previous night, and Donovan had spoken with them at length after the waiter had whispered something to him.

The taller man with the dark tinted glasses gestured to Mike. "Come in, please," he said with a heavy Spanish accent. "We had hoped we could have been done here before you arrived."

"What are you doing here?" Mike asked, surprise mixed with resentment in his voice.

"It should be obvious. We wished to search your room, and now that you are here, we will search you, too."

"I demand to know—"

"You are in no position to make demands," the man said gesturing to his companion with the gun. "As you can see, we have the advantage."

Mike did not like to be bullied, but for a brief few moments he analyzed his situation. All things equal, he was sure he could take on either of them in a scuffle. It was the gun that made the difference. Maybe the stocky guy would use it, and maybe not, but it would be foolish to try anything with the odds against him.

"What the hell do you want?"

"Over here... by the wall, please," the man said. "Let's try to avoid any unpleasantness."

Mike took a deep breath and glared at the gunman. The fellow stared back at him and finally gestured with a nod toward the wall. Reluctantly, Mike moved beyond the bureau.

"Face the wall, please. Your palms on the wall."

Mike did as he was told and then he felt the gentle pressure of the gun barrel in the small of his back as fingers removed the wallet from his hip pocket, his handkerchief, a few dollars in bills from his left trousers pocket, and the change and keys from the right.

"All right, Carmen."

The pressure of the gun left as the stocky man stepped back. Mike straightened up and watched the other man inspect his wallet.

"Mr. Michael L. Barnes," he said, reading from a business card. "You are an attorney?"

Mike nodded. He accepted the wallet when the man had finished with it, and watched him put the bills and change on the bureau. The man picked up the stack of tourism pamphlets. "Are you here as a tourist?"

"Yeah."

The man then lifted an envelope. Mike knew it was the note from Harlow that was left for him at the desk the night he checked in. He had tossed it in a drawer where it was out of sight. Now he thought about Harlow's words of caution.

"This," the man went on, "is a note from Donovan Harlow and tells you to *say* you are a tourist." He tapped the envelope thoughtfully on his fingers, his eyes narrow and suspicious. Then he tossed it aside. "It would seem as though you came here from New York purposely to see Mr. Harlow."

"That's what you think."

"You spent the evening with him last night, apparently as his guest. And this afternoon you visited him at his apartment."

"We were in the Army together."

"But you came here purposely to see him?"

"Did I?"

The man considered the answers, and by his expression Mike hoped he had not pushed back too hard. Carmen stood silently by, the gun in hand but it was no longer pointed in Mike's direction. Then the first man moved to where Mike's clothes were hung and made an inspection. "Tell me, Mr. Barnes," he said in a calm tone. "Do you have a coat with those trousers you are wearing?"

Mike did his best to appear unconcerned, but the reminder jolted him inside as he remembered where he had left the jacket... with the souvenirs in the pocket. But he could make no connection with them and these two thugs.

"No," he said trying to be casual. "Why would I be wearing a jacket in this heat?"

The man with the gun – Carmen – spoke for the first time since Mike had come in. "Julio..." His eyes were busy scanning the room, weighting the truth of Mike's statement. "It could be true. There is no coat like that here." Carmen seemed a little nervous, wanting this mission to be finished.

Julio appeared to accept Carmen's conclusion. "A little

more cooperation, Mr. Barnes, please. We have not quite finished. Would you please step into the bathroom and close the door... so we don't have to watch you."

Mike knew that this polite, smooth-acting character was going to finish the job, one way or another, and that he'd probably use whatever force necessary. There was no reason to take any risk. "Sure," he said with a sarcastic grin, and slowly stepped toward the bathroom door. "Take your time... and let me know when you're through."

He pulled the door shut behind him and groped in the dark for the light switch. Listening intently, he could hear very little activity through the heavy door. What could this all be about? The two burglars certainly weren't seeking cash or jewelry – they had left at least two hundred dollars untouched in his wallet, and his *Rolex* remained on his wrist. As his confusion mounted, Mike tried to make sense of the whirlwind of recent events, but with little success. A few minutes passed, and he thought he heard a door close. After a few seconds of total silence, he cautiously emerged from the bathroom.

Julio and Carmen were gone. The suitcase had been replaced to its original location, the bureau was clear and the drawers closed, and everything appeared as if nothing had been disturbed at all. Mike stepped out the front door, but the balcony walkways were deserted. As he returned to the room a little smile crept across his face, and with it came a certain feeling of respect. Still confused, though, he had to admit that the pair had carried out their mission with minimum unpleasantness.

But that feeling soon left him when he remembered his jacket. He hurried to the elevator, and when he reached the lobby floor, be casually walked to the lounge entrance as not to draw any attention. When he saw that his sport coat, unfinished drink, and cigarette pack were still as he had left them, he did not return to the table right away, but instead, made a tour of the atrium. When he was quite certain that his recent visitors were no longer there, he went back to the table. As soon as he lifted the jacket from the chair, he knew the souvenir boxes were still in the pockets. He finished his drink, threw down a ten-dollar bill on top of the check, and returned to his room.

Chapter 5

This time when Mike Barnes returned to his room, he engaged the dead bolt lock, pulled the boxes from his pocket and placed them on the small table in front of the windows. He threw his jacket in one chair, sat in the other and stared at the two boxes.

With all possibilities of reasonable explanations for the room search exhausted, Mike opened the smaller of the boxes and removed the St. Christopher medal. There seemed to be nothing significantly unusual about the piece, so he put it back in the box, and then removed the cigarette case from the larger box. It still seemed just as ugly. He fondled it a few moments and then snapped it open, exposing the tissue paper inside, and the smaller, tissue-wrapped objects packed under the top layer. Aware that this was not how he had last seen it, he removed several of the small pieces and unwrapped them. Green fire flashed back at him from the first object, a glimmering stone that he figured must be an emerald. As he continued, an array of twenty or more rubies, sapphires, emeralds and diamonds lay on the table before him. Lips pursed tightly, his thoughts reverted back to his original impressions of Donovan Harlow, and maybe those impressions weren't so inaccurate after all.

For the moment he forgot about Julio and Carmen who had violated his privacy. At the forefront now was his concern that he had been deceived by an unscrupulous and clever mind. Confident that he had recruited an honest accomplice, Harlow had tricked him with the emotional approach that he knew Mike would fall for, especially because of his sense of obligation. Donovan could be sure that the case – in Mike's hands – would arrive safely in New York. He'd shown Mike the tissue-filled case, and then sent him to another room in search of the box. During that short absence, the gemstones were packed, already individually wrapped for that purpose.

Who the recipient was in New York and where the gems were to go, at this point, did not matter to Mike as he repacked the stones, and returned the case to its box. A little resentful anger churned inside him as he got out of his clothes and went into the bathroom to shower and shave. The concept continued to aggravate him while he dressed, and by that time he was convinced that Harlow's story had been false in every way. He didn't believe there was a wife... or a son... nor had there ever been. Now he was quite certain, too, that even the thirty-thousand-dollar check would prove to be worthless.

It wasn't until he was riding down in the elevator with the two boxes in his pocket that he realized another stroke of luck had brushed his shoulder: had it not been for his determination to find Lori McKay, the case and the gems would now be in Julio's possession.

The Royal Palace was quite busy when Mike arrived at seven forty-five. Most of the tables were taken, but there was a space at the bar. He stood there gazing about until Perry, the bartender, came to ask him what he would like to drink.

"Is Donovan here?"

"No, sir, he isn't," Perry said. "Haven't seen him yet this evening." He stared inquiringly at Mike as if to repeat the drink question.

Mike ordered a glass of wine that he didn't want and sat there until Eduardo Espinosa noticed him there. The maitre de came over at once, bowed in his precise, stiff little way and said, "Alone tonight, Mr. Barnes? I have a table... if you are ready."

"Actually, I was looking for Donovan."

"He left word that he would not be in until later."

Mike had no choice but to accept the information. Because he didn't know how long he would have to wait and because he knew he would have to eat sometime, he slid off the barstool and followed Eduardo to a table at the front of the room. Eduardo graciously pulled out a chair for him and presented the menu that seemed to always be under his arm. "If you like shrimp," he told Mike, "I can recommend them highly." As his guest sat down and opened the menu, he added, "Enormous... seven or eight to the pound. Flown in fresh from the Gulf."

"Okay," Mike agreed. "I'll try it."

Espinosa wrote on his pad, tore off the sheet and handed it to a passing waiter. Mike sipped his wine. He thought he was in no mood to enjoy gourmet food, but when it arrived, he found he was hungry when he started to eat. The shrimp was truly enormous and more succulent than any he remembered. He ate everything, and when the waiter returned, he asked for more coffee.

He didn't see Bridget Palmer come in, but somehow she was there at his table, blonde and voluptuous in her blue gown with the swooping neckline. He started to get up as a gentleman's gesture, but she smiled and said, "Please... don't get up. I'll just sit for a minute." Mike would have preferred to sulk alone, but he remembered his manners long enough to ask if she would like a drink. She ordered a Scotch and soda. While she sipped he asked if she would be singing again that night.

"I was here five to seven... during cocktail hour. Then I'll

43

be on from about nine-thirty to eleven-thirty."

"That's quitting kind of early for a place like this," Mike remarked.

"Oh, well, we close at midnight. This really isn't considered a night club." She thanked Mike for the drink, excused herself, and sauntered off to mingle with the customers at the bar.

Mike's impatience mounted by the minute. Periodically he glanced about the dining room and the bar. Somehow, Lori McKay had entered without him noticing, and not until she was standing at the back of the room talking to Eduardo Espinosa did he see her. But before he could get to his feet, she was climbing the railed staircase. When she started across the narrow balcony, Mike sat down again and watched her disappear beyond the office door.

For the next few minutes, Mike's thoughts were suspended in a series of visions, skipping from Lori to Harlow to the cigarette case full of gemstones to the two men, Julio and Carmen, who had searched his room. But right then, none of it fit together with logic or understanding. Unconsciously he watched Bridget having her second drink with some man at the bar. Then his eyes drifted to the string quartet, and finally, after what seemed like a half-hour, but in reality was, perhaps, five minutes, he headed for the back of the room, and then started up the stairs. Without any plan fixed in his mind, he had no idea what he would say or do, and as it turned out it made no difference because the office was empty.

This room was somewhat larger than Harlow's apartment office with desk, three chairs, file cabinets, water cooler, and a computer. But there were no closets or doors to other rooms – just the metal door connecting Harlow's apartment. Mike knocked. He knocked again. He pounded and listened, and then tried the knob. When there was no response from the other side, a lump of fear raced his heart into his throat. He spun on his heels and started down the stairs.

At the bottom, he found Eduardo talking to a waiter. "Eduardo... do you remember the young lady who went up to the office?"

"Certainly. She had an appointment with Donovan at nine. I explained to her that he wasn't here, but that he might be in the office or entertaining guests in his apartment."

"Do you have a key for the connecting door?"

"No." Eduardo shook his head. "Only Donovan has that key."

"I'm going to try his front door." Mike turned away and headed for the exit.

"But Donovan must be there. The girl could not have entered through the office. Perhaps—"

Mike Barnes never heard what Espinosa had in mind. He hurried out to the street. The half-block to the corner was just a blur of bright lights and crowded sidewalk. Then it was behind him as he turned left onto the darker side street, moving with long strides and finally breaking into a run. When he turned left again at the corner, he noticed a silver Mercedes pulling away from the curb halfway up the block, but his interest was more focused on the arched doorway about fifty or sixty feet ahead. He didn't wonder about the light cast from the entrance of Harlow's building until he was near enough to see that the door was open. Had he not known Harlow better, the open door wouldn't concern him. He stepped into the foyer and bounded up the flight of stairs. At the landing he found the apartment door ajar, and without hesitation he pushed it wide open. Barging inside, he stopped abruptly, gasped, and froze where he stood. Now he knew why he had felt that sudden urge back in the restaurant to take action.

Donovan Harlow lay face down on the living room floor, and even then Mike could see the dark stain widening and discoloring the hardwood beneath the light-weight blazer. He stood there for several seconds, horrified, unable to move until the initial shock of the discovery had passed. He could feel the beads of sweat trickle from his forehead, and he was conscious of his labored breathing and the clammy dampness of his shirt clinging to his back. Even though the room was hot and still, a cold shiver tingled his spine as he forced himself to move closer to the sprawled body.

He kneeled, pulling at a limp shoulder, not thinking whether or not it was right, turning the body over in an attempt to discover some sign of life. It was then he saw the front of Harlow's shirt saturated dark red, and two distinct holes in the fabric. His palms were wet with perspiration, but as he felt for a heartbeat, the bare skin he touched seemed as warm as his own. Quite certain that there was no pulse, he forced himself to accept the fact that the indestructible lieutenant of Delta Company was actually dead.

Then a small metallic click sounded from somewhere within the apartment that awakened Mike's perceptions. He had heard it clearly, but he couldn't identify it. There came some other sound, more muted and less distinct. His eyes were instantly busy as he got to his feet again, his imagination soaring. It was then he noticed the oil painting leaning against the baseboard. It had hung on the wall that afternoon, and now, in that space was the face of a small safe with a hole where the combination knob should be. Even from a distance Mike could see deep scratches and gouges around the hole, leaving the appearance that someone had knocked the combination off with a heavy hammer or chisel.

Instead of looking closer at the safe, he inspected the floor in a widening circle away from the body. He did not see a gun, eliminating the possibility that Harlow had taken his own life. But before he could wonder about what had actually happened, a new thought came to him and he froze. He remembered why he had come here – not because of concern for Donovan Harlow, but because of a girl named Lori McKay.

The thought of her fate shocked him. "Lori?" he called out, with his eyes focused on the dark bedroom. "Lori!"

In the eerie silence he stepped closer to the bedroom doorway, frightening thoughts strangling him. He strained his ears listening, but by the time he had reached the door, he had heard no other sounds. Feeling along the wall beside the door, his fingers found the light switch. With a click the room was bathed in brightness. A quick scan first noticed the open barred panel and window, and then that the spread was missing from the king-sized bed.

Remembering the clicking noise he had heard, he stepped to the window, inspecting without touching the hinged steel bar grate on the inside that was secured with a latch that was now unfastened. He thought this could have been the source of the noise, and if not, perhaps the metal door between the offices. With his handkerchief wrapped around his fingers, he swung the grate open wider and leaned through the open window to look down into the dark space between this building and the next, recalling the alley and the gate he had noticed that afternoon.

It was then that he heard another sound, this time a sort of muffled pounding. It seemed to come from the general direction of the bathroom. He found Lori McKay when he opened the door, standing as if waiting, her face white with shock, fear streaming from her green eyes. Her hair was all mussed, and she held the corner of the bed spread in one hand, the bulk of it on the floor at her feet. Mike felt a sudden rush of relief. He reached for her arm and stepped closer. "What happened?" he asked. "Are you all right? Are you hurt?"

She shook her head, her body surrendering to his grasp. "No," she whispered. "I don't think so." She looked up into Mike's eyes, bewildered. "There was no one in the office, so I knocked... and someone opened the door."

"Who?"

"I don't know."

"Was it dark in this office?"

"Yes, but there was light in the front room."

"So you stepped inside."

"I didn't realize, then, what I was doing until someone grabbed me from one side, and then this came over my head and a hand clamped over my mouth."

"A man's hand?"

Lori nodded. "Strong... I tried to twist it away, and I felt a large ring."

"Then what happened?"

She looked at Mike's eyes, hesitating. "I just don't know. I'm not sure if something hit me, or maybe I just fainted, but the next thing I knew, I was on the bathroom floor with this thing over my head, and something tied around my arms."

Mike saw the twisted shower curtain that had been yanked down and used as a rope. He led her into the bedroom and made her sit on the bed, wondering how to tell her about Donovan.

She listened without interruption, her cheeks still pale and her eyes wide. Mike kept his story brief and to the point, and as he spoke, he felt grateful for her understanding and self-control, and he thought how wonderful she seemed to him. When he finished he told her to stay there while he called the police.

He got the desk light on and pushed aside the restaurant menu that partially covered the phone, but when he reached for the phone, he hesitated. For some reason unknown to him, he opened the door connecting to the restaurant office, went through without a glance and hurried down the steps from the balcony in search of Eduardo Espinosa.

Chapter 6

Acrime of this nature was immediately turned over to the Homicide Squad. Although a number of uniformed policemen arrived first to protect the scene, the man who headed the group of investigators that arrived a few minutes later in answer to Espinosa's phone call was Captain Quinten Vincennes, a slim, neat man of about forty-five, graying hair, quick and observant eyes, and a quiet but commanding speech. With him came his chief detective, Arthur Reynolds, fingerprint and evidence specialists, and a photographer. Not far behind was the medical examiner from the Dane County Coroner's Office.

Vincennes politely instructed Mike Barnes, Lori McKay, and Eduardo Espinosa to remain in the bedroom while the investigators made their initial inspection, took photographs, and the deputy coroner examined the body. Over an hour later, they saw the ambulance attendants remove Donovan's body on a gurney through the front entrance, and a short time later Captain Vincennes came into the bedroom. He considered each of the three thoughtfully, as though he was deciding how to proceed.

"The safe was found open," he said. "Obviously a forced entry. But we're not sure when... that is, before or after Donovan was killed. It's quite possible that the perpetrator was caught in the act of breaking into the safe and silenced Donovan Harlow for good." With raised eyebrows he stared at the three, each in turn, as if to prod for some voluntary comments. When there was no answer, he went on. "Well, there was nothing of great value inside," he said looking at Espinosa, "but I find these agreements quite interesting. You know about them?"

"Yes," Espinosa responded. "And I can explain why they were made." He unbuttoned his tux jacket, shifted his weight and rested his hands on the chair arms. It was then that Mike saw the heavy gold and onyx ring on the third finger of his left hand. He glanced quickly at Lori, but she seemed not to have noticed the ring, so he said nothing.

"When I came from Portugal," Espinosa said, "I learn quickly that I, a foreigner, would have difficulty entering into business here. I am a hotel and restaurant man... that is my profession. I have some money, but not nearly enough, and it was impossible for me to obtain a loan. So, in order to start the sort of restaurant I have in mind, I need a..." He groped for the right word, gesturing with both hands.

Mike supplied the words. "A silent partner... an investor."

"Exactly." Eduardo acknowledged the assistance with a nod. "I look around the city at all the available establishments and make inquiries, and the name Donovan Harlow is suggested as one who might help me. So we meet and discuss the matter and arrive at an agreement."

"And the business prospered," Vincennes said, "and you shared in the profits."

"Well, for my part, I took a very large salary. But a few weeks ago, my copy of the agreement was stolen from my room. I'm quite certain that Donovan Harlow is responsible."

"Without it," Vincennes said, "you had no claim on the business."

"That is true."

"Also, by the terms of these agreements," Vincennes went on, "the survivor comes into possession of the business should one partner die." He glanced up at the husky figure of Reynolds who stood by making an entry in his notebook from time to time. He looked back to Espinosa. "This has now happened."

"I was in the restaurant all night... if you are suggesting that I am a suspect."

"We don't know yet, exactly what time he was killed."

"But if I had killed him, I would have taken the documents, yes?"

"Perhaps. But a clever man might leave an open safe, the valuables gone, and the documents left to be discovered later, so he would appear innocent, as you wish to be, and the business would fall into his possession."

Mike Barnes viewed Captain Vincennes with new respect. And then he remembered the cigarette case pressing against his chest in an inside jacket pocket. Had he been smart, earlier he had the opportunity to get rid of the case. It would have been simple to just put the case in a desk drawer before the police arrived. They could have discovered it and drawn their own conclusions, leaving him free of any suspicion.

Once the police discovered the case, it would provide all the motive they needed for a murder like this. There could be little hope for the truth to be accepted. Even he found it difficult to believe the story about Donovan's son, so how could he expect the cops to go along with it? He sat there mentally grasping at straws as Vincennes directed his attention to Lori.

"You came in at nine o'clock, Miss McKay," the captain said. "You had an appointment with Donovan Harlow that you made earlier by phone. What time was that?"

Lori thought a moment. "A little before six."

"And he agreed to see you at nine."

"Yes."

"What did he say?"

"He told me it would be easier to find the restaurant, so I

was to come to the office, and if he wasn't in, I should knock on the door connecting to his apartment."

"Is that what you did?"

Lori nodded and related again the events that led up to Mike finding her in the bathroom.

Vincennes nodded when she had finished. He paced to the doorway to the living room, stared for a long moment at the open safe, and then came back. Standing directly in front of Lori with his hands clasped behind his back, he bowed his head slightly. "Had you recovered consciousness, perhaps, in time to hear a shot?"

"Two shots."

"Did you hear anything else? Voices? Scuffling?"

"Well, just before the shots, I heard a man's voice... but I'm not sure what he said."

"Try to think," Vincennes prodded. "Was it in English?"

"Yes." Lori hesitated, brow wrinkled and lips trembling. "It sounded like... *'Don't... don't be silly.'*"

"And then the shots?"

Lori nodded and tears stained her cheeks.

Vincennes considered her answers, nodded, and then he digressed to an earlier time. "I understand you arrived here last night on a train from New Orleans. Did you travel alone?"

"Yes... well, I shared a compartment with an older woman. She and her nephew had a chauffer waiting at the depot in Columbus, and I came with them to the hotel in Madison."

Mike recalled the man and older woman he had seen through the open door of the room on the eighth floor, and now he understood why Lori had gone there. He watched her as she replied to the detective's questions; he liked the way she conducted herself, controlled, even though there must have been a bit of fear deep inside. She had spirit and resilience, and though he had known her only a few hours, he felt proud of her.

Vincennes continued. "The purpose of your trip was to see Donovan Harlow? Why?"

"He owes my father twenty-five thousand dollars. He's ignored all our letters about the note that's past due."

"Your father sent you to collect this debt?"

"Actually, it was my idea. His health isn't good, and he couldn't make a trip like this."

"And have you ever been in Madison before?"

"Oh, yes... we lived here when I was growing up." The rest of her story came easily as she explained that her father had been a civil engineer for the city, and that she had lived here until her mother died just after she turned seventeen. Then she had lived with an aunt in Ohio while she went to college. When her father reached retirement age, he had invested his savings in a partnership with Donovan Harlow, and moved to New Orleans where he ran their small shipping company.

An expression of surprise suddenly came to Vincennes' face. "Is your father Leonard McKay?"

Lori nodded. "Yes. Do you know him?"

"I knew of him," Vincennes said. "I remember him speaking at several city council meetings. But I didn't mean to interrupt. Please go on."

"Well," Lori continued. "My father and Donovan Harlow bought an old freighter. They hauled miscellaneous cargo, but mostly bananas from South America."

"Donovan Harlow," the detective said, "was a partner in many things... not all successful. This note you mentioned... did it have to do with the ship?"

"A year and a half ago, Dad's health started to fail, and his doctor said the stress was too much for him... that he should get out of the shipping business and try to relax. Mr. Harlow bought out his share. Paid partly with cash and the rest with a note for twenty-five thousand."

"Your father was a trusting man."

Lori brushed the hair back from her forehead, and Mike noticed a little red color come to her cheeks. "At the time, he didn't have many options."

"Thank you, Miss McKay," Vincennes said politely. "We'll need a written statement covering all the details from you later." Then he turned to Mike. "You came to Madison to see Donovan Harlow, too." It was a statement rather than a question.

Mike Barnes shook his head. He had already decided that it wasn't time, yet, to tell everything. "No, I came here on a vacation. I was having difficulty shaking a bronchial infection, and my boss in New York suggested I take a week off and get some country air. I'd never been to the Midwest, so I booked a flight. Donovan and I were in the same Army unit in Iraq, so naturally I looked him up."

"You were close friends?"

"I wouldn't call it *close*. With Army buddies it's different. When you're visiting a strange place, you don't have to be a *close* friend to look him up."

Vincennes seemed to accept the reply. "And in your talks with him since you arrived, did he mention anything about leaving Madison in the near future?"

Mike thought for a moment about the conversation he had overheard earlier that day. "I did hear that subject come up in a conversation he had with his pilot." He appeared to be trying to recollect any other statements Harlow had made, but in reality, he briefly considered the two men – Julio and Carmen – who had searched his room. They certainly had hoped to find the jewels, but why they had suspected him to have them, he did not know. To bring this up now would only pose the question of how he knew of the stones. And until he knew the truth about them, if they even figured into this equation, he decided to withhold the information. Instead he told Vincennes about the three visitors who had come here that afternoon during his meeting with Harlow.

Vincennes listened intently, his dark eyes bright with new interest. "This pilot he referred to as his partner," he said. "Was this a rather big man with blonde hair?"

"Loud clothes that didn't match. Needed a haircut."

"When they talked at the door, did he sound threatening?"

"His tone of voice implied that... yes."

"Crawford," Vincennes said to his partner, Detective Reynolds, and then they stepped into the living room where they whispered a brief conversation. Reynolds turned to one of the other detectives, whispered something to him, and the other detective left the room through the front entrance.

Vincennes returned with more questions. "The woman who showed up next... you said her name was Celeste?"

"I think that's the name I heard."

"And the man who followed? Can you describe him?"

"Harlow called him 'Major.' Small man. Gray hair."

Vincennes paused in though for a few moments, then turned to Reynolds again. They whispered another brief conversation; Reynolds relayed orders to another detective.

When the second detective had left, Vincennes removed a long envelope from an inside jacket pocket and lifted the flap, glancing at each of his three witnesses, looking for a reaction, as he revealed a large number of new hundred-dollar bills.

"We discovered this taped to the back of a desk drawer," he said. "The contents of the drawers had been rifled, but maybe there hadn't been enough time for a more thorough search. Nine thousand dollars. Kinda suggests that Harlow didn't completely trust the safe." He returned the envelope to his pocket, stepped over to the doorway to give the safe another look, and then came back to stand beside Reynolds. "It's rather surprising," he said to no one in particular, "that there are no diamonds." He eyed Mike and Lori. "It was known that Harlow bought and sold gems... diamonds, mostly." He shrugged, as if dismissing the thought, and then focused his attention once more to the three witnesses. "I must ask you to come to the station where we'll take your written statements. We have cars waiting outside."

"Are we under arrest?" Mike asked.

Vincennes eyed him curiously. "No... but in a matter as serious as this, it's in our best interest to take your statements there... in a controlled environment."

To Michael Barnes, Vincennes seemed to know a lot about Donovan Harlow and the people with whom he associated. Perhaps it was because Harlow was more of a public figure here than Mike realized, being a popular restaurant owner. But the detective's secretive manner puzzled him, and now that he knew the gems were more than likely a part of this scenario, a seed of panic found a place in his mind to sprout. As he, Lori, and Espinosa were ushered to the front door and down the stairs, he had time to grasp an understanding, and to estimate more fully the odds against him. Deep down he didn't believe he could be convicted of a crime he had not committed, but if Harlow's gems were discovered on his person now, after he had failed to disclose their possession, he would certainly be considered the number one suspect. He could hardly expect the police to overlook such an obvious detail, nor could he expect them to believe the truth, at least during their initial investigation.

As a lawyer he also knew that most murders did not remain a mystery and were solved in a relatively short time once the facts were known. And then it was a matter of apprehending the true suspect. It seemed likely that when Vincennes had gathered all the facts, he would know who killed Harlow. What Mike wanted to accomplish was to eliminate himself as a suspect, but unfortunately, he was holding some very discerning evidence. And because he had not taken advantage of the opportunity to get rid of it, he would have to risk the truth to explain why he had the jewels.

Because the gems were Harlow's and now a part of his estate, and certainly of great value, his conscience wouldn't allow him to just throw them in the gutter – even though he probably would get away with it in the dark – to be picked up by some undeserving, dishonest individual, and perhaps lost forever.

Briefly he entertained the idea of walking away when he reached the bottom of the stairs. Technically he wasn't under arrest, and although he knew he would be found again, perhaps it might afford him the time he needed to temporarily hide the cigarette case where he could recover it at a later, safer time.

But he was unfamiliar with the area and he had no idea where to go. Even if he could manage to dispose of the case, his abrupt absence would be looked upon as evasion; it would only serve as an element of guilt. No. His best option was to cooperate, and hope that the truth would prevail.

The trip to the modern-looking building took only a few minutes. Mike reached down to give Lori McKay's hand a gentle, reassuring squeeze as they marched through a long corridor. She smiled up at him. It was not a happy smile, but it was friendly.

They turned left into a large reception room where along one wall next to the windows were two desks, one occupied by a uniformed officer, and the other by a plain-looking woman busy at a typewriter. The earpiece indicated she was probably transcribing a recorded interview. On the other side of the room sat several people on chairs, and Mike realized that Vincennes' men had not been idle. Among those people were the man he knew as the Major and his wife, Celeste, Bridget Palmer, and the pilot, Abe Crawford.

Captain Vincennes directed Lori McKay and Eduardo Espinosa to chairs near the uniformed officer at the desk. To Mike Barnes he said, "Come with me." They entered another adjoining office with Detective Arthur Reynolds on their heels. The air-conditioned coolness would have been refreshing had Mike been in a mood to appreciate it.

Vincennes went directly to a chair behind the desk, shuffled some papers aside, and folded his hands on the desktop. He glanced briefly at Reynolds, and then smiled curiously at Mike, sitting in the chair in front of the desk. "Why didn't you run from all this when you had the chance?"

"Because an innocent man has no reason to run."

"And a clever, guilty man might try to convince us he is not guilty with that same tactic."

Mike knew he had gone as far as he could without the whole truth. He took out the cigarette case, the box with the St. Christopher medal, and Donovan Harlow's thirty-thousand-dollar check, arranged them in a neat row on Vincennes' desk, and then stepped back to his chair. "This is part of it."

Vincennes watched him closely, considering the items on the desk, and then nodded to Reynolds. "Would you object to a more thorough search?" he asked Mike.

"Not at all," Mike responded. "But if it's a gun you're expecting to find, I'm sure you know you're wasting your time."

"Yes, I know that. Let's just say it's a formality."

The detective sat back and watched his partner complete the search of Mike's clothing. When it was finished, Vincennes leaned forward and inspected the contents from Mike's pockets – wallet, handkerchief, ball-point pen, hotel room key, rental car keys, and some loose change. But he became more interested in the other items Mike had placed on the desk, perhaps because Mike had volunteered them. He opened the box, removed the gold medal, and laid it on the desk. Then he briefly studied the check, and then tapped the ugly cigarette case with his index finger. "I'll bet you're going to tell me the significance of these things," he said dryly to Mike.

"Open the case," Mike replied. "The contents will explain my concern."

Vincennes opened the case, pulled out the top layer of tissue, then pulled out and unwrapped one of the green gems. With a curious frown he continued to unwrap more of the stones until they were all spread out on the desk and the case was empty.

With nothing better to do during all of this, Mike counted the stones – twenty-four in all. He wondered about their value, and if Harlow had acquired them legitimately.

"So..." Vincennes said abruptly. "Were you delivering the gems to Harlow? Waiting for his check to clear?"

"No."

"Then, where did they come from."

"Harlow gave me the case."

"When?"

"This afternoon."

"Why?"

"He said it was a souvenir gift for another Army buddy of his. Wanted me to take it to him in New York."

"And you agreed to do it?"

"I didn't know about the gems inside it then. I'll tell you the whole story, and then you'll know I didn't kill Harlow."

Vincennes nodded and gestured toward a microphone at the edge of the desk. "I must remind you, Mr. Barnes, that all of this is being recorded."

Mike acknowledged, "I'd be disappointed if it weren't."

"I want you to start at the beginning," Vincennes said. "I will interrupt you from time to time if I feel the need for more detail, but I want everything in your own words, Mr. Barnes."

What Mike Barnes had to say took quite a while. He started with the background and his wartime association with Harlow. He explained the man's heroism and the obligation that he had felt during the following years. When he came to the more recent events – the trip from New York and subsequent phone calls and conversations with Donovan at the restaurant and in the apartment – Vincennes interrupted periodically to be certain of all the details, his surprise well masked until Mike told about the man with dark glasses and his gunman accomplice. New interest sparked in Vincennes' eyes as he interrupted to ask more about them.

"They spoke with a strong Spanish accent; they were dark-complected," Mike explained. "I'm quite certain they are Mexicans."

"Why do you think they searched your room... and you?"

"I don't know... unless they thought I had the jewels."

"Why should they think that you were carrying them?"

"They obviously knew I was a friend of Harlow's. They could have seen us together at the restaurant, and they probably suspected I'd come here to see him."

"But if they were after the jewels, they would've gone to Harlow."

"Maybe they did. You said yourself that you didn't know when the safe was knocked open."

"It could've been earlier... say, this afternoon. When they didn't find the stones, they came looking for you."

"Could be."

"And except for the fact that you left your jacket in the cocktail lounge, they would've succeeded." Vincennes leaned back, his eyes reflecting distance as he plunged into deep thought for a few moments, and then leaned forward again. "A strange story," he continued, "but believable to someone who knew Donovan Harlow. I knew him, and he was of the character you describe."

Mike felt a grain of relief to hear Vincennes refer to his story as *believable.*

Vincennes went on. "If he operated outside the law, it was never proved, although we always had some suspicions. We knew that he was buying gems – not that there was anything illegal about that. I suspect that some of the stones were smuggled in from South America. Some smuggling across borders is bound to occur in such a business, and Harlow, knowledgeable of gems and their values, bought them as investments." He paused a few moments to study Mike's reactions. "Of course, there were other things, too, but I think matters were getting difficult for Donovan Harlow. The shipping firm Miss McKay's father once ran is no longer of much value. And we found out that he was negotiating a loan on the restaurant, something that Eduardo Espinosa may have learned."

"In other words," Mike said, "Harlow was taking out all the cash he could so when he skipped town there wouldn't be anything left after the creditors took over."

"It was going to happen soon, too." Vincennes tapped on an envelope on his desk. "This is an airline ticket in his name. He had a reservation on a flight to Miami... day after tomorrow."

Mike stared across the desk. "But he told me he was going to Minneapolis, and then New York."

"A lie. Just like the story he told you about his son." Vincennes tapped on the envelope again. "Donovan Harlow was a gambler. He probably knew he was being watched, and he needed to get those gemstones to New York. He needed a courier he could trust. That's where you come in."

"But if I had been caught – like I almost was – he would have lost the whole works."

"True," Vincennes agreed. "But as a gambler, he made a wise choice. Except he didn't figure on Martinez recognizing you as his courier."

Mike threw Vincennes a curious glance. "Who?"

"Julio Martinez... one of the men who broke into your room. We know of him, too, but I didn't expect to find him involved in this. It's just not his style."

"Captain... if you don't mind me asking, who is this Martinez? And what is his style? Should I be concerned?"

"Julio Martinez is a known drug dealer. The D.E.A. has been building a case on him for a couple of years. They're just waiting for the right opportunity to collar him, and maybe a few of the others working with him. He's usually the mild-mannered type, a mechanic in a truck shop, the last person you'd expect to be violent. But why he has an interest in Harlow's little box of jewels, I have no idea."

Reverting back to the current situation, Vincennes touched the gold medal again. "This part was clever. Asking you to deliver the cigarette case to a stranger might make you suspicious, but with the story about his son and this medal to prove his devotion, you wouldn't doubt him. Yes... very clever, indeed." He began putting the stones back into the case. "I'm sure we will find this check to be worthless, too."

He slid the case, the St. Christopher medal, and the check into a large brown envelope, placed it on a table among other items tagged for evidence, and then turned to Mike. "For now," he said, "I will accept the statement you've given, but I must warn you that you are still considered a suspect. We'll talk to the others now, but you'll have to wait in the other room. I will want to talk to you again after the rest are gone."

Chapter 7

Vincennes did something then that Mike thought rather unusual: instead of calling each of the other witnesses into his office separately for private interviews, he stepped into the outer office after Mike.

Mike's eyes found Lori McKay. It helped his morale when she smiled at him and stepped over to speak to him in anxious tones. He could detect her concern as her green eyes darted about his face, inspecting every detail. There was doubt and uncertainty, but not suspicion, and it was somewhat comforting that her concern seemed to be for him. "I'll explain later," he whispered, reassuring her.

Vincennes moved behind the desk that the uniformed officer had just vacated and announced to the group that he was about to check the statements each of them had made, and that there might be a few questions, after which they would be free to leave. He shuffled the papers around, and picked up one of the statements that had been transcribed. After a few moments of inspection he looked at Bridget Palmer. So did Mike, wondering just why she should be here at all until he heard some of her replies.

"You came to this area nearly two years ago, Miss Palmer," Vincennes said. "You were an entertainment director at a resort."

Bridget was leaning against the back of her chair, poised, bare arms folded across her breasts, her head up and gaze steady, alert. "That's right," she replied.

"You were discharged after less than a year's employment. Why?"

"Is that important?"

Vincennes considered the response and decided it was

not. "You then came to work for Donovan Harlow. How did that happen?"

"The house band used to let me do a song with them once in a while. Donovan felt bad – sorry for me, I guess – when I got fired. He said I could work for him, so I did."

Vincennes scanned the second page of the statement. "You were asked about some women's clothing we found in Harlow's bedroom closet, and you admitted they're yours."

"Yes, I told you they are."

"But you say you left them there more than two months ago."

"It's more like three months."

"You haven't been in the apartment since then?"

"No." Her painted lips twisted and she gave Celeste Barbary a quick, scornful glance. "I no longer amused Donovan. He told me so," she added bitterly.

"You were not in that apartment this evening?"

"No. I've told you that three times."

"At nine o'clock you were in the restaurant?"

"Yes."

"Did you see Mr. Espinosa at that time?"

"I saw him around. I didn't keep track of the time."

"He could've been absent for a few minutes?"

"I s'pose he could have."

"And you say that you saw nothing out of the ordinary that might help us."

"That's right."

Vincennes quickly glanced around the room at the other witnesses. The only one to notice he did it was Mike Barnes. "Very well," the detective said blandly. "You may go."

Bridget seemed surprised that her act was over so soon, but she lost no time in getting out of the room.

After consulting his next set of sheets, Vincennes looked straight at Abe Crawford. "You left here on Sunday in your DC-3 with miscellaneous cargo. You state that you stopped for fuel in Houston, and then took off again, headed for Guatemala. But you only got as far as Veracruz where you had engine trouble. You left the plane and returned here last night, but not on a scheduled flight."

"I told you," Crawford said. "I got lucky. I got a ride."

"From Veracruz?"

Crawford hesitated, his eyes suddenly shifty and his voice a bit surly. "No," he said bluntly. "Look, it's all there in my statement. Why do I have to— "

Vincennes waved him to silence. "Don't be impatient. We can verify what you've said in your statement. When we find out what plane brought you here, we'll know where you came from."

He studied the statement again for a few moments. "You threatened Donovan Harlow this afternoon."

Crawford swallowed hard and leaned back in his chair. "Who says so?" he asked, his eyes glowing with defiance beneath the mussed blond hair. "Donovan and I had a deal, and I wanted my cut before he high-tailed it out of town."

"What do you know about him leaving?"

"I'd just heard that he was. I wasn't taking any chances. I told him I'd be back. If you want to call that a threat... okay."

"And you did return this evening?"

"Sure I did. I said so. But not by nine o'clock. If Harlow was killed around nine like you say, I was riding a bus then... somewhere between my place and downtown."

Vincennes waved his hand, dismissing Crawford. The pilot, too, wasted no time in leaving. When the door closed, Vincennes picked up another of the transcribed statements, focused his attention on it a few minutes, and then turned to Eduardo Espinosa. "I have scanned over your statement," he said. "Is there anything you can add to this?"

"Nothing I can recall right now," Eduardo replied.

"You didn't leave the restaurant until Mr. Barnes came to tell you that Donovan Harlow had been shot?"

"No, sir."

"And the only people you saw use the balcony stairs were Miss McKay and Mr. Barnes?"

"If there was anyone else, I did not see them."

Standing like a statue, his arms folded across his chest and his eyes narrowed to just slits, the detective finally told Espinosa he could leave. Then in a more polite, considerate tone he turned to Lori McKay. "Miss McKay... I don't think it will be necessary to detain you any longer unless you have remembered anything you want to add. I'll read your statement later."

Lori shook her head and nervously fidgeted with her handbag. "I can't think of anything," she said. "But I did tell you that I thought the man who held me wore a ring. I just noticed that Mr. Espinosa wears a ring, and so does Mr. Crawford."

Vincennes smiled. "As does Major Barbary, I see. Very well." He escorted her to the door.

At the desk again, he added Lori's statement to the stack, selected another, and then, after briefly looking over the report, stared at Celeste Barbary. She wore navy blue satin slacks with a dazzling white blouse, sitting erect without stiffness, and appearing cool and unconcerned, her hands at ease in her lap. To Mike, the way she held her head and the calmness in her eyes, made her seem even more regal-looking than ever.

"You had dinner with Donovan Harlow this evening at Houlihan's Restaurant," Vincennes began. "Then you drove back to Harlow's apartment, arriving there at five minutes to nine."

"I think it was about then, but I couldn't swear to it."

"It couldn't have been much later," Major Barbary cut in, "because she was home by ten after nine, and I don't think she could drive that distance in much less than fifteen minutes."

Vincennes nodded, but continued to watch the woman. "You left Donovan Harlow on the sidewalk in front of his door?"

"Yes, I did."

"You didn't get out of the car?"

"No."

In a quiet, almost apologetic tone, still not shifting his stare, Vincennes said, "Excuse my asking this question, Mrs. Barbary, but were you having an affair with Donovan Harlow?"

"Nothing of the sort." The reply came quickly and with no signs of emotion. "I liked Donovan. We were friends. I would occasionally meet him for dinner or a drink."

"With your husband's knowledge?"

"Not until recently."

"With his consent?"

That question brought out a little color in her cheeks. She glanced sideways to her husband. "Quite the contrary," she said, and then took a deep breath. "My husband is a jealous man. He has old-fashioned ideas, and we don't always agree."

"You came to the apartment this afternoon to warn Harlow?"

"I came to the apartment." She looked at Mike and took her time to continue. "Mr. Barnes was there."

When she did not elaborate on the reason for the afternoon visit, Vincennes turned to Major Barbary. "You followed her, Major?"

Orlando Barbary had been watching his wife. He folded his arms across his chest and glared at the detective, his jaw jutted and his lips pursed tightly beneath a neatly trimmed mustache. "I did."

"According to Mr. Barnes," Vincennes went on, "you threatened Harlow."

"Yes, and I meant to."

"If he continued to see Mrs. Barbary you were prepared to act."

"Damn right I was," the Major said explosively.

"You might've used a gun."

"I might have."

"But you didn't."

"No."

"While your wife had dinner with Harlow, you stayed home?"

"All evening."

"It would help if someone could verify that statement."

"I'm aware of that."

"Were you aware that Harlow intended to leave the country? Were you suspicious that your wife might leave with him?"

Barbary unfolded his arms and put his hands on his knees. He leaned forward stiffly. "I've had about enough of this," he snarled. "I've told you what I know. My personal matters, in my opinion are none of your business. If you think otherwise, then arrest me and see where it gets you."

Mike noticed that Vincennes was irritated with the Major's outburst, but that he remained surprisingly calm. He nodded to Mr. and Mrs. Barbary. "Thank you for coming in," he said politely. "I will be in touch with you tomorrow."

When the door closed, Captain Vincennes sat at the desk and shuffled the stack of papers as if to merely do something to occupy the time. Then he stood and sauntered over to the other desk where the transcriber remained busy, as she had been the whole time. He peered over her shoulder at the typed page for a few moments and then returned to address Mike Barnes. "Your statement will be ready to sign shortly."

"Then what?" Mike asked. "After I sign it, do I get to sleep at the Marriott? Or do you have a cell waiting for me here?"

Vincennes smiled. "Considering the circumstances, Mr. Barnes, I should hold you until we have had time to verify your story. But for some odd reason, I believe you, and I won't hold you now. But I will advise you *not* to leave town." Then his smile diminished to a frown. "For that same odd reason, I don't think you will, but, of course, we will alert the airlines not to honor your ticket back to New York until further notice. I'm sure you'll understand."

Mike didn't offer any protest; it seemed useless.

The transcriber stepped over to Vincennes with several typewritten sheets. He took them from her, dismissed her to her usual office, and began scanning each page. After some time he said: "It seems that Harlow devised a very thorough plan. He had you arriving back in New York on Saturday. The jewels, I would guess, would've been delivered to someone at the airport as soon as you arrived, and being the weekend, you weren't apt to discover the worthless check for at least a couple of days. By that time he could have been out of the country."

Mike nodded and agreed that it was a safe assumption as Vincennes handed him a pen and the typewritten statement for his consideration and a signature.

"Take all the time you want," the detective said pointing to a table across the room. "When you're finished, you can pick up your personal belongings."

Fifteen minutes later Vincennes walked with Mike to the door. "You did a foolish thing tonight, withholding that information for so long. I hope your story proves to be the truth."

Mike nodded.

"I'll have someone drive you back to your car. We'll be in touch." He opened the door. "Good night, Mr. Barnes."

There were several people in the hallway, but Mike saw only the attractive girl on the bench, who rose at once and smiled at him. "Is it all right? Can you go now?" Lori McKay asked.

Because this was just about the nicest thing that had happened to him in the past twenty-four hours, Mike had a difficult time answering. The fact that her concern had prompted her to wait for him struck a spark within him that quickly became a warm glow and strangely blocked his ability to speak. He grinned at her, happy she was there, and tried to forget all the troubles.

"Come on," he said when other words wouldn't come. He tucked her hand under his arm and they strolled toward the front entrance.

Chapter 8

There had been a bright moon earlier, but it had settled behind the city skyline when Mike Barnes and Lori McKay came down the steps to the sidewalk. Without even thinking about his next course of action Mike stopped and just stared at the girl, still impressed with her concern for his well being. It was then he heard a man's voice call his name from the doorway. Vincennes had instructed a patrolman to drive him back to his rental car that was parked near Harlow's apartment.

"Will it be alright if Miss McKay rides along? Mike asked. "I'll be giving her a lift back to the hotel."

"I don't see a problem with that," the officer replied as he directed them to a police cruiser parked just around the corner. He politely opened the rear door for them, as would a chauffeur. They climbed into the seat and settled back, sitting close, their arms touching.

For a second or two Mike considered slipping his arm around Lori's shoulders; somehow it seemed the right thing to do and he had the feeling she wouldn't mind. It wasn't bashfulness that made him hesitate, but instead the simple understanding that their being together was truly something wonderful, and he didn't want to spoil it with such a brave act so soon.

Once in his rental car again and finding his way across town, without prompting he found himself telling Lori everything that had happened. He didn't give any thought to their mutual aloneness and the exposure to trouble that had brought them so close, but he did recognize the feeling growing inside him that this was his girl, like he had known her for a long time.

She listened intently, glancing his way from time to time so he could see the soft curves of her face and the brightness dancing in her eyes in the intermittent glow of passing streetlights. By the time they reached the west side of Madison they were sharing their thoughts, wondering and speculating about who had killed Donovan Harlow, but found no answer. Later, cruising along the Beltline Highway, she spoke of her father.

"Was he a ship pilot?" Mike asked.

"Yes, until he was forced to retire."

"Oh?"

"Dad went to New Orleans after he left his engineering job here in Madison, but retirement didn't agree with him. He couldn't be idle, so he took to traveling some, and that's when he met Harlow down in Panama. They struck some sort of partnership deal and together they bought that old freighter... started a shipping company. Dad agreed to manage the operations, and because of his Navy experience he fit right in as the captain of the ship. He really enjoyed it, too, and everything went along fine until he had a mild heart attack. When he recovered, the doctors told him he couldn't do that sort of work any longer, and that he should return to his home in New Orleans. Harlow paid him some of the money for his share and gave him the note for the balance..."

Her voice trailed off, and when she didn't continue Mike asked: "What does he do now?"

Lori chuckled softly. "He couldn't stay away from boats and the water, so he bought this little marina on the inland waterway in Florida, and he's having a wonderful time running it. But it needs some improvements. That's why the twenty-five grand is so important to him."

"He'll get it now," Mike said, and when he saw that Lori

didn't seem to understand, he explained. "All those gemstones are a part of Harlow's estate. They're bound to be worth ten times what he owes your father. The estate executor will have to pay the note when this mess gets straightened out."

"Yes," Lori said thoughtfully. "I suppose you're right. I hadn't thought of that."

It was nearly 3 AM when they reached the hotel. At that hour, the bar and restaurant on the main floor were closed. It seemed by then that they had run out of conversation anyway, and Mike understood why – they were both tired. Lori's dull reactions indicated sleepiness, and she was very much in favor of getting some much-needed rest.

When they left the elevator on the third floor Lori opened her purse to find her key. Abruptly she stopped.

"That's funny," she said. "I'm sure I had it with me."

Back at the main desk the clerk retrieved a duplicate key, and again they rode up to the third floor and started along the balcony. Mike took the key from her as they neared room 306. He unlocked the door and swung it open, Lori at his side as he stepped in and reached for the light switch. The door snapped shut just as he flipped the switch, but no light came on. He tried it again, and still nothing happened. It was then that instinct and quick reflexes jolted him to action. Any other time he might have blundered forward in search of a lamp, but recent occurrences had made certain impressions. Violence and murder had already conditioned his senses, and in an instant intense fear tore at the ragged edges of his nerves. There was no sound in the room, yet a vivid premonition of danger lurked in the darkness. Although the room remained obscure, the drapes were pulled back and against the starlight of the night sky something moved. He didn't know what it was and he didn't take time to speculate. Even with all the blackness closing in on him he remembered the layout of his own room. With one hand clamped hard around Lori's waist he turned to the left and thrust into the darkness and the bathroom door that should be there. Lori gave a soft cry of surprise as his lunge took them sideways. Mike felt and heard something drop to the floor. Just then another dark movement caught the corner of his eye. Simultaneously there was a flash and the vicious boom of a gunshot as they spun, half falling through the open doorway. With his free hand he slammed the door shut behind them. When he had regained his balance he quickly reached for the doorknob and pushed the lock button. Then in absolute darkness they stood there, silent, Mike's one arm still holding Lori close. He could feel the pounding of her heart, and then he realized it was in sync with his own.

Several minutes had passed when he realized how tightly he was holding her. He relaxed his arm. She drew a deep breath, and she, too, loosened her firm grip on Mike's arm. For another few seconds they stood silently still, and from somewhere outside Mike thought he heard a door close. When there was no further sound he released her and stepped back. But Lori's hands found him again and pulled him close.

"No," she whispered urgently.

"I think I heard a door close."

"Don't go out there yet," she said softly, as though she sensed his desire to investigate. "It could have been a trick."

"All right," he replied. "We'll wait a bit, but I don't think he'll stay long after that shot."

The silence was broken only with their breathing. After a minute or two Lori spoke. "I guess someone really did take my key, Mike."

"Yeah," he responded.

"If I had come here alone— "

Her voice shuddered, and Mike spoke quickly, not wanting her to dwell on that thought.

"Where was the key?"

"In my bag."

"Where is the bag?"

"I dropped it outside the door."

"Who could've taken it out of the bag? Eduardo sat next to you during the ride down to the police station."

"Yes."

"Who else had a chance to grab it after we got there... while you were all in the room together... while I was in the other office with Vincennes?"

She thought a few seconds. "I don't know. I left it on a chair next to me most of the time. I just didn't pay any attention."

"Yeah," he said, and then in a delayed reaction of fear, he felt himself start to tremble. Nerves ragged and strained, sickness grew in him. Until then the action had kept his mind busy, but now he understood clearly that in someone's twisted thoughts there was still the promise of more killing. Among the five other people who had been questioned at the station, one had come here with a gun – probably the same gun that had taken Donovan Harlow's life.

He tried desperately to discard the thought, not wanting to pursue it or consider the reason for this attempt. He flexed his stiffened muscles and felt the cold perspiration on his spine. Unable to stand still any longer, he gave Lori's hand a little squeeze and gently pushed her away. "Stay right here," he said. "I'm going to have a quick look. Don't turn on the light."

Lori's whispered protest went unheeded as he cracked open the door. He was startled into stiffness again when he heard a loud pounding knock at the outside door.

He opened the bathroom door wider. "Yes," he called out.

"Security, sir," a man's voice replied.

"Just a minute," Mike answered, assured now that the danger was past. He flipped the bathroom light switch and stepped out to the entrance doorway, opening it partway.

A large man in a black suit stood in the lighted balcony corridor. "Sorry to bother you, sir, but did you, perhaps, hear anything that might have been a gunshot?" he asked.

Mike hesitated in thought. Vincennes should know about this, but he saw no point in trying to reach him now. As for the security guard, or the hotel manager, for that matter, an explanation to them could accomplish nothing.

"Gunshot?" Mike said, making it sound rather ridiculous.

"Yes, sir. A lady called from another room, said she was awakened by a loud noise. Thought it sounded like a gunshot."

"No," Mike replied. "I didn't hear a gunshot."

The man touched his forehead as a sort of salute. "Okay. Thank you. Sorry to bother you, sir. Goodnight." He walked away.

When Mike closed the door, he saw Lori standing in front of the bureau, another lamp not controlled by the switch by the entrance turned on. She was holding a key. "He must've left it here."

"Who?"

"Whoever was just here. It was on the bureau, and I'm sure I didn't leave it there."

For a moment Mike wondered if there might have been

fingerprints, but it was too late now that Lori had handled it again. He walked past her to the lamp that was controlled by the switch at the door. It instantly came on as soon as he tightened the light bulb in the socket. Then he stepped toward the windows to examine them, still trembling with the thought of what might have happened if he had not escorted Lori to her room. Satisfied that no one could have entered by the window, he turned and faced the girl as a new thought came to him. He tried his best to disguise his fears with pretended cheerfulness.

"Those people who came here with you from the train," he said. "Did you know them before?"

Lori stared at him, puzzled. "Why, no. Mrs. Flagstone was good enough to share her sleeper compartment with me. There was none left when I got my ticket."

"And the young man?"

"Daniel... he's her nephew. They're traveling cross-country to Seattle, making several planned stops along the way. I think she said the next one would be Minneapolis."

"Just tourists?"

"I believe so. Why?"

Mike smiled at her. "Forget it. It was just a thought... that maybe you could have left your key in their room earlier."

"No," Lori replied. "Because I used it to get back in."

Mike took her arm and walked her to the door. "When I leave, be sure to lock the deadbolt, and hook the security chain, too."

"I will."

"Maybe we could go for a swim in the morning, and then have breakfast... not too early, though."

"I'd like that," Lori said, sounding like she really meant it.

"Then I'll just wait for you. Come by my room when

you're ready." He leaned toward her and gave her a little kiss before opening the door. "The latch," he said again, reminding her. He pulled the door shut and waited until he heard the deadbolt click and the security chain rattle. Then he started down the corridor toward the elevator, still shaking inside and his cheerfulness gone.

Chapter 9

Mike Barnes didn't wake up until shortly after nine that morning, and when he opened the drapes he saw that it was a clear, bright morning with just a few wispy little clouds here and there. At first the events of the previous night were still hazy in his mind, but he remembered the date he had made with Lori. It pleased him to dwell on it, and the anticipation began to work on him. He breathed deeply and watched the traffic below him on the Beltline Highway.

A knock on the door surprised him. He grabbed his bathrobe and slipped it on as he crossed the room. Expecting Lori but wondering why she should be this early, he opened the door to find the blond and busty figure of Bridget Palmer standing there. She smiled as she made a brief survey of his robe and pajamas, which didn't seem to bother her at all. Before Mike could recover from his surprise, she said "Hi," and strolled past him in her snug-fitting sundress. She didn't stop until she reached the windows. Mike followed out of curiosity, and when he stood beside her she said, "Some view, huh?"

"Yeah," Mike replied.

She opened a small shoulder bag and produced a pack of cigarettes and lighter. When Mike refused her offer, she lit one for herself, replaced the pack in the bag, and then plopped the bag onto the small table in front of the window.

Mike eyed her cautiously, knowing she had come here at this hour for some purpose, but she was taking her time to voice her intentions. He wanted to get her talking. "So... did you always live here?"

"Heavens, no," Bridget replied. "I'm originally from

upstate New York."

"And you were an activities director at a resort here? How did that happen?"

"It was more like a glorified lifeguard at a Wisconsin Dells water park. And if you really want to know the truth of the matter, I think it was just a publicity stunt on the part of the owners."

Mike's eyes were filled with questions.

"You see," Bridget went on. "When I first came here from New York, I had been hired to be in the cast of the Tommy Bartlett water ski show. But that was seasonal, of course."

Mike nodded his understanding. He was noticing that her blond hair was expertly done, and although there was, perhaps, a bit too much make-up, there was a certain prettiness about her face, and he thought her figure was still good, even though she was starting to show a little heaviness in her hips and thighs. But exercise, and a few weeks of lifeguard activity instead of working out at a piano might cure everything.

He saw, too, that she was well aware of his inspection, and it seemed to amuse her. "But," she continued, "I got to meet a lot of people. I knew this fellow, and he knew someone else." She gestured with her cigarette. "And that someone else was affiliated with a big hotel and water park. They decided to hire some of us from the show for their indoor facilities that operated year-round. I thought it was a good idea, so I took the job."

"When did Donovan enter the picture?"

Bridget considered the question for a moment or two. Her smile faded.

"He had a standing reservation at the hotel. He spent a lot of time around the pool playing poker. At times I didn't have much to do – keep an eye on the women and children, hand out towels now and then... you know, sort of a handy Mary." She turned to grind out her cigarette in the table ashtray.

"Frankly, it was pretty dull. Plenty of men to buy you drinks and dinner, but easy to get in the habit of not being around when I should've been. Anyway, they gave me the axe."

Mike decided he might as well get personal. "By that time I guess you were in love with Donovan."

She put her arms on the windowsill and leaned on them, her gaze fixed on the horizon. "S'pose you could call it that," she said without emotion. "I bought his line of charm, but in the end I sort of got short-changed. If I'd just gone back to New York for the winter I'd have been much better off." She sighed audibly and dismissed the matter. She was ready to get to the business that had brought her here. "What time did they let you go last night?"

"I think it was after three when I got back here," Mike said, a little puzzled with the abrupt change of pace. "Where were you then?"

"In bed. Where do you think I'd be?" She looked at him, her head slightly tilted. "Are you in the clear?"

"Not exactly."

"They give you a rough time?"

"Rough enough."

"Would it be worth something to know you were clean?"

"Sure it would," he said, not yet understanding what she was getting at.

"How much?"

Now Mike knew the score. Bridget meant exactly what she said, and yet there was an instant when he couldn't quite accept his conclusion. He simply looked at her, momentarily stunned. With a conscious effort he kept himself in control, even as the anger began to churn inside him. "You know something. Is that it?"

"Maybe."

"Why not take it to the police?"

"I may have to."

"But you'd rather have cash."

"Let's just call it a favor. I do you one, you do me one."

Mike started to speak, then thought better of it. He felt his eyes burning and his jaw muscles tighten. "If you know I didn't kill Harlow, then you know who did."

"No," she replied. "I don't."

With anger warping his judgment, he nearly spoiled his opportunity. He had in mind to phone Vincennes and let him take over. But just in time he understood that would accomplish nothing. Without a witness she could simply deny she had made any such proposition. This was no time for anger. It was, though, the time to stall, to play along, until he could gather a few more facts.

He remembered the noise he had heard when he was kneeling beside Harlow's dead body – that metallic clicking sound that came from another room. He recalled the barred windows, and at the time he had thought someone had escaped that way. Bridget? He didn't think so, because it had been a man who grabbed Lori in the darkness.

"So, what's your price?" Mike asked abruptly, hoping to catch Bridget off-guard. "How much do you want, and what do I get for my money?"

She was caught off-guard. She had, perhaps, expected him to protest, so she could just walk away, creating a little panic and increasing her odds. "I'll let you know." She tucked her bag under her arm, turned and started across the room. Mike moved with her, and just before she reached the door he grabbed her arm and pulled her to a stop.

"Why not now, Bridget?" As he spoke he could see the change in her. Maybe it was his uncompromising gaze that was so unlike his usual mild manner. Or it might have been nothing more than her desire to quit while she was ahead. Whatever the reason, she seemed eager to get away. Her eyes were anxious and uncertain as she slipped from Mike's grasp.

"I just wanted to be sure how you felt," she said in a brooding tone. "There's no hurry, is there? We can both think it over, and maybe later— "

She didn't have time to finish before someone knocked. A step ahead of Mike, Bridget opened the door to find Lori McKay standing there in bathing suit and robe, her face smiling in that first instant. It took her only that long to see Bridget, and a pajama-clad Mike. The sparkle in her eyes abruptly turned dim and the smile dissolved. "Oh," Lori said in quiet astonishment. She backed up a step. "I'm sorry." She started to turn away.

"Come on in, honey," Bridget said. "I was just leaving."

"Lori!" Mike called out, but he was talking to an empty doorway. When he moved past Bridget, Lori had already stepped into the elevator and the door was closing behind her.

Bridget studied Mike for a moment. She shrugged her shoulders. "Sorry," she said, unhurriedly stepped to the elevator door and pressed the down button.

Chapter 10

Mike had his breakfast in the coffee shop. He thought it would be quicker than room service. As he ate, he considered his immediate problem. He wanted more than anything to find Lori and tell her what had happened. But time might be important, so he resigned himself to postponing the explanation. Bridget's visit and proposition had opened up new possibilities and he wanted to explore them if he could.

It wasn't that he expected to solve a murder. That was a police job and they had the knowledge and equipment to do it. Somehow, he couldn't be concerned with his own involvement anymore. But he couldn't forget what had happened in Lori's room. The deadly flash of a gun in the darkness and those moments of terror remained vivid in his memory. Someone had intended to kill Lori. He didn't know why, but the terrifying fact remained: that someone, having failed once, might try again. Maybe if he could discover a clue as to the reason, perhaps he would know how to prevent it. And right now, he couldn't just hang around the hotel like a disciplined schoolboy. Later, when he had done what he could, he intended to stick to Lori McKay like a leech.

Instead of going back to his room, he used his cell phone to call Quinten Vincennes. He had a little difficulty reaching the right department, but finally a woman's voice informed him that Detective Vincennes was not in. Mike left his name and said he would try again later.

Crossing off the number one item on his mentally inscribed itinerary, he considered number two. Law office experience told him that next to the police, a newspaper was the best source of information. Scott Newman had impressed him in their brief meeting and he was sure Newman could tell him many things. Mike had a good wedge to stick in the door: his knowledge of the murder, and his own implication. It seemed that an exchange of information might be mutually helpful. He headed out to the parking lot to his rented car.

The offices at the *State Journal* seemed less crowded than they were the first time he had been there. Like a newspaper man with his nose always pointed in the right direction, Scott Newman spotted Mike as soon as he approached the counter. He backed out of his little cubicle and came over to offer a handshake, his intelligent dark eyes reflecting the sincerity of his welcome. "Just the man I want to see," he said. "I hope you're here to tell me about this Harlow business."

"I thought you'd already *have* a story."

"We do, but we could always use more."

"Can you get away? Is there someplace we could go to get a cup of coffee?"

"Sure. C'mon. I'll take you down to my private club."

Scott Newman's private club turned out to be a little beer garden pub and café a couple of blocks from his office building. They went around to a side entrance into the restaurant and bar area. Off to the right was a small dance floor and riser for a band, and beyond that was the exit into the open-air beer garden with a dozen or so tables, several potted palm trees, and a variety of colorful tropical plants.

It was here that Newman spent part of his free time, and he explained the merits of the place after he ordered two coffees: the food was good and cheap, and it was convenient. "Sort of a poor man's Royal Palace."

Mike stared quizzically.

"You know... food and music and dancing where you can

leave your dinner jacket and formal gown at home."

Because there were questions he wanted to ask, Mike had already made up his mind to tell Newman what had happened. He instinctively liked the man, and he recalled what his co-worker in New York had said about him. A Canadian; an ex-RAF pilot with a hankering to write and a little newspaper training; a bachelor of thirty-eight, tired of the cold Canadian winters; he was marking his time in Madison until he was ready for bigger things. He seemed like a man Mike could trust, so he proceeded to tell the story with minor deletions, emphasizing first that since it was unofficial and mostly confidential he didn't think there was much that Newman could use in print.

He omitted the part about the attempt on Lori McKay's life, but he included his own interest in the case by saying he was still under some suspicion, that he would prefer to get back to his job in New York, but that it was unlikely that any such permission would be given until the case was solved.

"So you're doing some snooping," Newman said.

"Sure. Donovan Harlow and I were Army buddies. I certainly didn't kill him, and I want to learn what I can so the cops don't invent some reason that I did."

Newman considered Mike's sincerity. He, too, was feeling that mutual sense of trust and friendship. "If you should get lucky I guess you'd tip me off, so what do you want to know?"

Faced now with the need for something concrete, Mike was not sure where to begin. In the back of his mind was the idea that he might stumble across some new information, something, perhaps, regarding the backgrounds of those involved that would give him a lead, or suggest a motive. "I guess Harlow's the key," he said. "I know about the partnership in the South American freighter, the restaurant, but not much about the partnership with Abe Crawford. What do you know about that?"

Newman thought a moment while he sipped his coffee. "Not a lot of detail. Crawford started the service with a couple of Cessnas and a part-time mechanic. In fact, a long time ago, I wrote some ads for his charter service. He flew vacationers to the resorts in Mexico. It wasn't big business, you understand, but he made a living at it. He might have done better if he'd had a little more ambition and a little less affection for the bottle."

"When did Harlow enter the picture?"

"I can't be absolutely sure about that, but I think they've had some affiliation for many years... since before Harlow went to the Gulf. It's obvious that they must've made some partnership arrangement, because Crawford could never have bought a DC-3 on his own."

"He would need a co-pilot to fly a DC-3, wouldn't he?"

"He had one until about a week ago."

"I understand he flew south on Monday."

Newman shrugged. "If he did, it wasn't with the co-pilot I knew. This lad was another Canadian, and he went back home."

Mike thought it over. "Do you think Harlow and Crawford could've been mixed up with drug dealers? I mean... transporting for them?"

"Sure," Newman replied. "But it goes farther back than that."

"What do you mean?"

"Back in the eighties, before Noriega was captured, Crawford was suspected of gun-running to Panama, but he was never caught."

"Where did the guns come from?"

"Don't know. Texas, probably. They were flown into secret landing strips in the jungle. Crawford had just the kind of aircraft to do it."

"The DC-3?"

"No. The smaller Cessnas." Newman hesitated as he gazed around the room. "I remember a piece the *New York Times* ran back then. I can't quote it, but it told about a secret airlift allegedly smuggling guns and ammunition from Texas and other areas of America into Panama that was under investigation by a Congressional committee. The idea was that this supply of weapons was for planned revolutions in Latin American countries.

"I don't know how much truth there is in the possibility of Harlow and Crawford actually being mixed up in any such business. Harlow never flew the planes, so I guess he could have been involved without even knowing it. They contracted cargo and passengers, and if the money was there, I doubt if he'd ask many questions."

"Sounds like it could have meant a nice little profit for Harlow."

"Quite a little! Then, after the Panama crisis cooled off, Harlow got into diamond dealing, but I think that might have just been a cover for the coke trade."

"Oh."

"Yeah. The banana boat out of Columbia and Brazil was the perfect opportunity, don't you think? And then the planes to distribute the stuff to wherever here in the States."

A waiter poured their third refill of coffee. Mike was intrigued by what he had heard, and not at all surprised by Donovan Harlow's enterprise. But the information itself led him nowhere, so he tried for another angle. "Do you know Bridget Palmer?"

Scott Newman thought a moment. "Oh, sure. She was somewhat a celebrity... in the Bartlett Water Show up in the Dells. Somehow she got to hanging around with Harlow and she got fired from a hotel job up there. I think that's when she started singing at the Royal Palace, and I guess she even lived with Harlow, until just a couple of months ago, as a matter of fact."

"If she was bitter enough about a break-up," Mike said, "and if she got herself in the right sort of mood, and if the opportunity presented itself, she might have shot him."

"It's possible," Newman said. "There's no telling what a woman might do in that situation." He took another sip of his coffee. "But somehow, she hardly seems the type. Never impressed me as being the hotheaded sort."

"She doesn't seem like the type to be lonely too long," Mike said. "Has anyone taken Harlow's place?"

"I've heard that Abe Crawford helped to comfort her," Newman chuckled.

Mike was amazed that Scott Newman seemed to be quite well-informed about the people associated with Donovan Harlow, so he was still hoping to stumble onto something unknown to him so far. "Do you think he might've given Bridget the brush because of Celeste Barbary?"

"That I don't know. Reports are that they've been seen together, but I'd be inclined to suspect her husband more than her. Don't know anything about him except that he's got some sort of engineering job. And you said he came to Harlow's apartment yesterday afternoon with a gun— "

"I didn't see the gun," Mike interrupted. "It was just the way he kept his hands in his pockets."

"If he came once with a gun, and if he knew what was going on, he could've come back."

Mike repeatedly sipped his coffee, somewhat disappointed that of all the information he had heard, none of it seemed very important. He put down the cup. "What about Eduardo Espinosa? What do you know about him?"

"Only that he's done a bang-up job of running the Royal Palace."

"Portuguese?"

"I doubt it."

"He said he came from Portugal."

"I've talked with him. From his accent and other little things I've noticed, I'd say he's probably Columbian, although I couldn't be certain."

"Any political angles?"

"Hard to say, these days."

Mike nodded and then a new idea came to him. "Harlow had his fingers in a lot of pies, right?"

"He did."

"A guy as busy as he was with all those business deals would have a lawyer, wouldn't you think?"

"I would."

"Would you happen to know the lawyer?"

"No, but I could probably find out when I get back to the office." Newman glanced at his watch and pushed back his chair. "And I think I'd better be getting back."

Mike put his hand on Newman's shoulder to keep him from rising. "Maybe you could do one more thing." He paused to get his thoughts in proper perspective. The thought had been half-baked in the back of his mind ever since Bridget Palmer's proposition. It seemed that she was prospecting for the highest bidder for the information she claimed to have. Therefore it seemed logical that someone else – very possibly the guilty party – might also be approached.

"Do you have any friends in the local banks?" Mike asked.

Newman grinned. "I've got friends everywhere."

"Friends who would be willing to give you confidential information?"

"What do you have in mind?"

"I'd like to find out if any of the people we've been discussing made any sizable cash withdrawal today."

"Whoa!" Newman's grin faded. "You're a lawyer. You should know that banks are a little sticky about revealing that kind of information."

"Officially, yes."

"And this isn't official?"

"Not exactly."

"Is this really important?"

"I think it could be."

Newman rubbed his jaw and frowned. His gaze danced around the barroom and then settled on Mike. "I'll tell you what I'll do," he said, hesitating while he reconsidered his answer. "I do favors. Other people at the paper do favors. And we get favors in return. Maybe – just maybe – I'll get the information as a favor, but—"

Mike smiled at him. "I know exactly what you mean. I'm not going to introduce the information as evidence. What you're saying is that you will deny ever getting or giving such information. And your bank friend will deny it, as well. Understood.

"I guess that sums it up quite well."

"That's good enough for me," Mike said. "Because if it ever comes to a point of evidence, the police will go right to the source on their own."

"I guess you're right," Newman replied. "Let me get back to my office and I'll see what I can do."

They stepped out into the bright sunshine again, making their way up the street. "Where's your car?" the reporter asked.

"Parked out in front... the dark blue Mercury sedan."

"I'll meet you there as soon as I get the lawyer's name."

A few minutes later, much quicker than Mike expected, Newman appeared on the sidewalk. "Juan Delsoto," he said. "Here's his address." He handed Mike a slip of paper. "Call me later on that other matter. This may take a while. And if you should come up with something," Newman said, half closing one eye, "you know where to find me."

Chapter 11

Mike dug out the city map that he had left in the car for his first day of "tourism" in Madison. He quickly decided that he would stop at the Royal Palace first.

At mid-morning, the interior of the Palace was cool and dim and quiet. The tables were set for the luncheon clientele, but there were no customers yet. Mike was only mildly surprised that the place had not been closed out of respect for Donovan Harlow. He walked up to the bar where a young black man in a long white apron was dumping a large bucket of ice cubes into the built-in cooler under the bar. The lone bartender, the only other person there seemed to be preparing for a busy shift, and when Mike asked if it was too early for a beer, the man said "No. Local or imported?"

"Let me try something local."

The bartender produced a bottle labeled *Spotted Cow*. "Very popular here," he said as he displayed the bottle for Mike's inspection.

Mike nodded his approval. The bartender opened it and poured part of the beer into a chilled glass. When Mike had tasted it and found it good he asked if Eduardo had come in yet.

"No, sir," was the reply as the man peered at a small clock on the back bar. "He usually doesn't come in much before noon."

Mike nodded again. Now that he had established his personal acquaintance with the management it would be easier to move about the place freely. After another swallow of beer, he stood up and walked to the swinging doors and into the kitchen. It seemed small and cramped for a restaurant of this caliber, but the stoves and walk-in coolers and the rest of the equipment were modern and top notch. More important, none of the half-dozen men and women working there paid him any attention as he walked past them and a couple of storerooms on his way to the back door that led, as he suspected, to the alley separating Harlow's apartment from the blank wall neighbor.

The alley was only about eight feet wide, and when Mike stopped under the two grilled windows that he recognized as Harlow's bedroom, he knew it would be rather difficult to reach those windows to make an entry, however, the drop for anyone coming down wasn't that great. Similar windows marked the living room, and then he was at the heavy wooden gate, the top of which was a foot or more above his head. A hasp secured the gate, and at present only a wooden peg was pushed through the hasp to keep the gate shut. Mike removed the peg, opened the gate and glanced up at the sign that said "Private Property." A push button just below another smaller "Deliveries" sign beside the gate evidently alerted kitchen personnel of someone at the gate. The inside of the hasp loop was shiny in spots, which made Mike think that during the nighttime hours it was secured, not with the wooden peg, but with a padlock.

Driven by curiosity and several unsubstantiated thoughts, he chuckled out loud. It occurred to him that he was playing detective, and in this case certainly a waste of time. A man like Captain Quinten Vincennes would have already inspected the alley, windows and gate. He would have considered the possibilities, if any actually existed.

Mike's unfinished beer was waiting for him when he went back to the bar. He considered the handsome young bartender who appeared to be the accommodating type.

"Does Bridget Palmer come in for lunch?"

"Sometimes," the bartender replied. "Sometimes she comes in during the afternoon when it's not busy to practice her music."

"Do you know where she lives?"

The barman turned to the back bar and produced a telephone directory. "She's in the book. I think she rents a place out in Maple Bluff." He handed Mike a notepad and pen.

Mike found the address and jotted it down on the pad. While he was at it, he looked up Abe Crawford's address, too. He tore off the slip from the pad, thanked the bartender for his help, and swallowed the last of the beer from the glass. Leaving a five-dollar tip on the bar, he heard the young man say, "Thank you, sir," as he turned away.

The building where Juan Delsoto had his office was located in a less-than-classy part of town, a nondescript brick structure among a row of many the same. Only the placards beside the doorways offered any distinction, indicating who occupied the various offices. Delsoto's was the third from the corner, on the second floor. The stairway was narrow, dimly-lit, and the stair treads squeaked with each step. It even smelled old and musty.

A black-haired girl sat behind a desk reading a magazine when Mike entered the small reception room. "Good morning," she said with a strong Spanish accent, barely looking up from the magazine.

"Good morning," Mike returned as he took out his wallet. He removed one of his business cards and handed it to the secretary, pointing out his name in the lower corner, so she wouldn't confuse it with the firm name. "I'm here to see Mr. Delsoto. Is he in?"

She smiled and slid back her chair, stood, and then disappeared through a doorway behind her desk. When she returned, she held the door open and motioned Mike to enter. "Right this way," she said cordially. "Mr. Delsoto will see you now."

The short, stocky man who stood up behind the desk in the inner office put a smile across his broad face. His eyes were nearly as dark as his thinning black hair that was combed straight back. His light gray trousers had an expensive sheen and his short-sleeved, open-collar shirt looked like silk. Mike noticed the heavy gold ring with a blue stone as he offered his hand across the desk.

"From New York, Mr. Barnes? This is a pleasure. Please sit down, won't you?"

Mike sat where he was directed at the end of the desk. Delsoto sat down again, leaned back and displayed another smiling expression. "What brings you to Madison, Mr. Barnes?"

"I'm not here representing my firm," Mike explained. "I'm a friend – or *was* a friend – of Donovan Harlow."

"Ahh," Delsoto said, and considered his burning cigarette in the ashtray.

"I was told that you were his attorney."

"By whom?"

"A friend at the *State Journal*."

"Oh, yes. A few people there know me." He drew a small puff from the cigarette and put it back in the ashtray.

"Were you?" Mike asked when the silence grew.

"I acted for him in certain matters." Delsoto waved a little sideways gesture. "A very tragic occurrence, Mr. Barnes."

"But not particularly surprising?"

"Excuse me?"

"I mean, a man like Harlow must have had *some* enemies."

"Possibly." Delsoto looked Mike square in the eyes. "You knew him well?"

"We were in the Army together... in Iraq. He invited me here for a visit."

"On a business matter?"

"In a way."

"And what is it you wish from me, Mr. Barnes?"

His gaze pessimistic as he considered the question, Mike stretched out his legs. Although it was comfortably cool there, he could feel the perspiration along the sides of his head, left over from the outside heat and humidity. He reached for a handkerchief and mopped his brow and temples, knowing that he wouldn't get much help or cooperation from Jonathon Delsoto. He was annoyed with himself for even coming here at all. But as long as he was here, certain persistence demanded that he continue his questions as long as there were answers.

"I found Harlow last night shortly after he was shot," he finally said. "I was – and still am, I guess – under some suspicion, and— "

"But why?"

"Captain Vincennes can answer that better than I can. The point is... I learned something about Harlow's activities and his plans. I thought you might be able to give me additional information."

"You want to help the police?"

"Let's put it this way: Until the police find out who did kill Harlow, I'm not exactly free to leave town. You were his lawyer and— "

"Like I said before, only in certain matters."

"Did he leave a will?"

"Not that I am aware. If there is one, it wasn't drawn by me."

"If there is no will, who will administer the estate?"

"That would be for the court to decide."

"And if there is no other lawyer, it might be you."

"A possibility."

"Did you draw up the agreement between Harlow and Eduardo Espinosa?"

"Yes."

"According to Detective Vincennes, Harlow was negotiating a large loan on the restaurant."

Delsoto crushed his cigarette butt in the ashtray. Still not looking at Mike he said, "This loan had already been finalized and was ready for execution. It would've been signed today."

"So now Eduardo Espinosa gets the restaurant."

"It would seem so, yes."

"Did you hear any indications that Harlow was getting ready to leave town?"

Delsoto shrugged. "He said nothing to me."

"What sort of agreement was there between Harlow and Abe Crawford?"

For a moment the lawyer hesitated, his expression evasive. "I knew there was some agreement, but I don't know the particulars."

"That's funny," Mike said.

"Funny?"

"That you know all about the restaurant agreement, but nothing about the planes."

When Delsoto gave no reply, Mike thought he was getting nowhere, and he decided to crowd Delsoto a little. "It doesn't make any sense. If you don't want to talk, say so. But don't tell me you know nothing about the charter plane service.

You knew Crawford flew the DC-3 out on Sunday. You must know he didn't bring it back. So what happened to it? Did Crawford peddle it to somebody or..."

He let the statement dangle when Delsoto stood up, remaining calm, showing no irritation at all as he glanced at his wristwatch. Then he made it perfectly clear that he couldn't be pressured. "You will excuse me, Mr. Barnes," he said politely. "I have other clients to attend to. If you want to know about the planes and Mr. Crawford's activities, why not ask Mr. Crawford?"

Mike got up from his chair and let out a deep sigh, aware that he had accomplished exactly nothing. "Okay," he said dryly. "I guess I will." He left the office, went down the musty-smelling, squeaky stairs, muttering his disgust under his breath.

Chapter 12

The route that Mike took to Abe Crawford's address led along the lake for a short distance, finally turning onto a street lined with brick apartment buildings. Crawford's number stood near the corner, a drab, two-story with a center entrance.

Because he was in unfamiliar surroundings, he was paying close attention to everything, and that was how he happened to notice the two men apparently coming from Crawford's building. They got into a car parked nearby, and only when they pulled away did he get a glimpse of one of them. He recognized the driver's round, expressionless face with the dark glasses, the Spanish accented man who had conducted the search of his room the previous afternoon.

The car was gone by the time Mike realized he should have gotten the license number. He sat there a few seconds, thoughts racing, imagination rampant. Recalling Crawford's statement about riding the bus, he figured Abe didn't own a car, so there was no point in studying the other vehicles parked in the vicinity. He got out of his car and started across the street, convinced that those two men weren't here by coincidence. They had paid Crawford a visit.

With some hesitation Mike stepped through the doorway into a foyer with an entrance door on each side, and a stairway to the upper level. The door on the right displayed gold numerals 201, and just below was a card tacked to the door with the name: Abe Crawford.

Mike knocked on the door. When there was no answer, he pushed on the door and it snapped open easily, revealing semi-darkness inside. Instinct commanded him to stand in silence a few moments, his heart racing, his stomach doing jumping jacks, his thoughts recalling the last apartment door he found open. Then, as he took one slow, cautious step into the eerie stillness, he froze, his startled stare fixed on the .45 automatic in Abe Crawford's white-knuckled hand, and just inches from his face.

They stood that way, silent, unflinching, Mike scared into a cold sweat and Crawford with a glint of anger in his eyes. Not daring to move, Mike forced his gaze beyond the gun to Abe's expression. He tried to speak but he couldn't. Then the bright, menacing glints in Abe's eyes faded, brows relaxed from their satanic scowl. The muzzle of the gun dipped, and then fell to his side in a loose grip.

"Oh," he said tersely. "It's you." Then, as an afterthought, his tone still mean, he added, "I was hoping those bastards might have come back."

Seeing the weapon fall away from its aim at a spot between his eyes, Mike could breathe again. He swallowed the lump of fright in his throat, and moistened his lips. "You scared the hell out of me," he said, taking notice that Crawford wore only pajamas and slippers. The fabric on his left shoulder appeared blood-stained, and a shiny spot of fresh blood adorned a cheekbone.

Silent again, Abe walked through swinging French doors into another room. While he was gone, Mike casually surveyed the shabby dwelling. The only light came through two windows that overlooked the street, draped with thin, dusty-looking curtains. All the furnishings -- a sofa, four arm chairs, a floor lamp, and a coffee table cluttered with magazines -- looked as if they'd come from a second-hand store years ago.

Crawford came back carrying a bottle of whisky and two glasses. The gun was gone. He put down the bottle and glasses, and then picked up a wallet from among the clutter. After a quick inspection he stooped to pick up a pair of trousers from under the table. Faded and not too clean, Abe nevertheless treated them with care as he straightened them out, slipped the wallet into the hip pocket and carried them off to the bedroom. Mike heard the scraping of drawers opening and closing, and then there was the sound of running water. A few minutes later, Abe returned. The blood had been washed from his face, and he held a wet washcloth to his cheek as he poured whisky into one glass and then pushed the bottle toward Mike. "Those bustards," he said, and took a gulp from the glass.

"I saw them," Mike said. "They were just driving away when I got here."

Abe found a crumpled pack of cigarettes in the clutter, but when he couldn't find his lighter in any of the pockets in the trousers he had just put on, Mike produced a book of matches he had picked up at the hotel. Crawford touched the wet cloth to his cheek, inspected it, found no more blood, and put it on the table. He pushed a chair closer, sat down, his gaze distant. His uncombed blond hair looked even more unkempt, he needed a shave, and his eyes were puffy and dark, perhaps from the lack of sleep. Thinking about his occupation, Mike was glad he didn't have to fly with Abe Crawford.

"Was one of them a real smooth-acting character?" Crawford asked. "With dark glasses?"

"Yeah."

"And the other one short and heavy? Kinda round-faced?"

"Yeah."

"He had a gun. Those damned bastards."

"They paid me a visit at my hotel room yesterday."

"Oh, yeah?" Abe stopped abruptly as he was pouring

another shot of whisky. "What?" he said in disbelief. "They came to see you? What the hell for?"

Mike slipped out of his jacket and draped it over the back of the chair. He glanced at the bottle, decided against it, and then proceeded to tell about the search of his room.

Crawford got up from his chair, shuffled over to the front windows, peered out to the street a few moments and scratched his head. "I don't get it," he said. "What would they want from you?"

Instead of answering directly, Mike asked, "Did you know that Harlow gave me some diamonds and other gemstones to deliver to someone in New York?"

Crawford moved closer. "No," he said with a suspicious glare.

"You *did* know that he was a dealer, though."

"Sure. I've picked them up in... well, various places... and flown them here to him." He scowled and shook his head, as if he had missed some information somewhere along the way, and now he was struggling to catch up. His expression made Mike think that he was an accomplished actor, or that he really was as confused as he seemed.

Mike told him about the cigarette case and Harlow's fictitious son. Crawford's reactions, as the story unfolded, gave Mike the impression that all this was really news to him.

"You think they came looking for you because they thought you had the diamonds?"

"I can't think of any other reason," Mike said. "Somebody busted open Harlow's safe, and searched the place. But if Detective Vincennes knows who... or when... he's keeping it to himself."

He was about to ask Crawford if he knew why Julio Martinez had come here when there was a knock at the front door.

Crawford stood up, his gaze darting to Mike, to the door, and to Mike again. "Now what?" he said irritated. After some hesitation, he went to the door and opened it.

Quinten Vincennes, casually dressed but very neat in appearance, stood in the doorway, and his partner, Arthur Reynolds, at his side. They didn't need any identification or introductions. The detectives showed great interest as they stepped inside and saw Mike Barnes.

"Ah, Mr. Barnes," Vincennes said. "I tried calling you at the hotel, but you had already left." As he spoke to Mike, his eyes were on Crawford. He couldn't help but notice the wound on Abe's cheek. "You've had some trouble, Mr. Crawford?"

Detective Reynolds closed the door and took a position just inside. Abe returned Vincennes' stare and mumbled some obscenities. "A little, Captain," he said. "A couple of guys came in here and gave the place a going over. Wish you'd been here a little sooner."

The detective's eyebrows lifted as he stared questioningly at the tall blond man.

"They searched the joint... my clothes, my wallet. I got a little pissed and tried to kick 'em out. But the one guy had a gun and I got slugged."

"Do you know them?" Vincennes asked.

Crawford hesitated a little too long and then replied, "No."

"What did they want?"

"I don't know." He nodded toward Mike. "Barnes saw them leaving."

Vincennes shifted his stare to Mike.

"Same two searched my hotel room yesterday," Mike said.

Vincennes surveyed the room, and then his eyes moved

busily, scanning the coffee table and its contents, and then back to Mike. "Ahh... Julio Martinez and his amigo, Carmen. I think we will have them in custody before the day is out." He sat down in one of the easy chairs. "I have some questions for you, Mr. Crawford, and if you would prefer, we can ask Mr. Barnes to leave."

"What the hell do I care what Barnes hears?" Abe said bluntly. He turned another chair to face Vincennes and sat down. "Shoot," he said.

"You say you don't know the two men who were here?"

"That's right."

"But you know what they wanted."

"I didn't say that."

Vincennes shrugged. "We'll get back to that later. The reason I'm here is regarding the plane – the DC-3 you flew out of here Sunday. We traced it to Houston where you got fuel."

"That's right."

"You left there with cargo... *agricultural tools*."

"Yeah. So?"

"The next report of the plane's whereabouts is Veracruz, Mexico, where you claimed to have engine trouble and left it there."

Crawford just stared saying nothing, waiting to see how much more Vincennes actually knew.

"But the plane *didn't stay there*," the detective went on. "Your next stop was Costa Rica for fuel only. That would suggest your destination was Columbia."

"Is that a guess?"

"Not exactly. On Saturday a young man from Columbia arrived here on a commercial flight. His visa listed his occupation as a pilot. He left here Sunday with you, apparently as co-pilot, but he did not return with you."

Vincennes paused, waiting for comment from Crawford. There was none, so he continued. "You had a reservation on a Friday flight out of Bogota, Columbia, but that was canceled, and you arrived here Tuesday night on a private jet."

"I told you that," said Crawford, his eyes darting about nervously.

"But you didn't tell me that this plane came from Columbia."

"So what?"

"Mr. Crawford," Vincennes said, a sharp edge now beginning to show itself in his usually calm voice. "You are wasting my time and yours. I can't prove that you flew you plane to Columbia, but supporting facts strongly suggest that you did: a Columbian co-pilot; your return flight from there; the absence, now, of the DC-3. It is my contention that you flew it to some remote airfield outside official jurisdiction where you sold it, and perhaps its cargo. And I believe the *agricultural tools* were really cases of guns and ammunition. I happen to know there is a market there for such *equipment*."

Mike Barnes had been listening with great interest, following along with the detective's reasoning, and his calculations certainly seemed plausible. Drug trafficking originating in Central and South American countries had been a growing problem for as long as Mike could remember. But now that he was reminded, Mike recalled articles he had seen and heard just lately in the news about gun-running to those same areas, and recent stories about the FARC, a terrorist group in Columbia, corroborated Vincennes' statement. It didn't really surprise him to think that Harlow could have been a part of it. If Vincennes' theory was correct, such a maneuver would be a natural for a schemer like Harlow, who had never been greatly concerned with scruples.

Crawford's expression had changed, as if he could no longer argue the point. He reached for his cigarettes on the table. "Suppose you're right," he said. "What's the beef?"

"Excuse me?"

"Yeah. There's no law against selling a plane. We have a plane we want to sell. We find a buyer. We sell it."

"How much does a DC-3 go for these days? Four, five hundred thousand?"

"Not that old crate."

"Two or three?" Vincennes prodded.

Crawford didn't respond.

"Maybe more if the buyer had a special interest, not necessarily legitimate."

Crawford still didn't argue. He leaned back in his chair and inhaled deeply the smoke from his cigarette.

"I'm kinda wondering about that payment," Vincennes said. "I'm wondering how it was made, and to whom." He paused, watching Crawford's reaction. "You didn't trust Donovan Harlow completely, did you?"

"Not lately."

"And I suspect he didn't trust you."

Crawford just shrugged his shoulders.

"I don't think he would allow you to collect the payment for such a sale. I think it would've been done some other way, a bank draft, perhaps, given to a third party, someone the buyer trusted, to be paid only after the plane was delivered. And Harlow, assuming you would return from Columbia Friday night, already had plans to leave the country earlier that day, and he'd have the money for the plane – and its cargo – in his pocket."

Vincennes gazed about the room, and then focused on Crawford again. "But you came back sooner than he expected.

You had delivered the plane and you wanted your share. It's not certain yet whether he was actually paid before he was killed, but he kept putting you off with excuses. When you came to his apartment yesterday afternoon, in this man's presence..." he nodded toward Mike, "...the threats you made, I believe, had to do with the money he owed to you."

Crawford started to interrupt, but Vincennes held up his hand, commanding silence. "We've checked the bus lines," he continued. "They aren't too crowded at that time of night, and one driver did remember a big, blond man like you. Dropped you off at the Square about twenty minutes to nine. That's just... what? Eight or ten blocks from Harlow's place?"

"You're crazy!" Crawford exclaimed. "Why would I kill Harlow before I got my cut?"

"You may not have had intentions to kill," Vincennes said. "You may have gone there to search, or to offer another threat. And you may have shot when Harlow resisted."

Crawford jumped up out of his chair and circled the table, his tone sharp with anger. "I sure as hell wouldn't kill him before I got my money. I wasn't there. You'll have to prove that I was."

"I hope to do so," Vincennes replied. "Now, you still don't know why the two men came here?"

Crawford closed his eyes tightly and shook his head. "No," he said.

"Well, I do know about them, and I'm surprised you don't recognize them, unless, of course, Mr. Harlow had never introduced you. I'm sure they have used your services quite often... that is, you have transported certain cargo for them. In fact, I would guess they were expecting a shipment when you returned this time."

Vincennes paused a few moments, anticipating some

opposition, but by this time, Abe Crawford appeared as though he was no longer capable of presenting an argument. He said nothing.

"I'm sure they were greatly concerned about its safe arrival," the detective said.

There was still no argument from Crawford.

"Donovan Harlow did do business with these men," Vincennes went on. "They were seen conferring with Harlow at the Royal Palace on Tuesday night. It is quite possible that they saw you there, too. By Wednesday they were concerned because you were here but your plane and their cargo was not.

"I suppose they would've come to Harlow for an explanation. By that time they must have known their cargo was missing, and the money it represented, as well. It is my belief, though I can't be absolutely sure, that they searched Harlow's apartment after Mr. Barnes left. I believe they broke open the safe. I believe they were looking for something of value as collateral until they could collect what was due them—most likely the diamonds—they knew he was a dealer.

"We know they didn't get the diamonds, but that was due only to luck. Knowing that Mr. Barnes was a friend of Harlow's and that he had just recently arrived, they went so far as to search him and his room, too. But you, Mr. Crawford, have no idea why they came here?"

"No," Crawford said.

"Well," Vincennes continued. "They probably hold you partly responsible. They came here hoping to find the money, or a bank draft, that must have been paid to someone here for the sale of your plane."

Mike listened with growing admiration for the detective and his powers of reasoning. He had asked his questions and let Crawford talk, and with a few facts and certain assumptions he painted them into a scenario that had solid possibilities. Mike knew now that he was seldom fooled for long.

But Vincennes was in no hurry. He was working at his own pace, without great pressure, possibly because he was dealing with an incident that crossed the line into a friendly country and wanted no diplomatic overtones. When Vincennes had the necessary evidence, though, he would move swiftly and with deadly aim. Crawford seemed to sense this. He was less confident when he finally spoke.

"Look, Captain," he said. "Your guys searched this place last night. You didn't find any money or any bank draft. Go ahead and search it again if you want to."

Vincennes gave a little smile. "I don't think that'll be necessary," he said. "I think those two who are worried about their cargo made a mistake. I don't think you have the money or the draft, Mr. Crawford." He walked over to the door, and Mike moved to join him. "I'll talk to you again, after we've completed our investigation at the Royal Palace."

Reynolds opened the door and stood aside to allow Vincennes and Mike lead the way out and down the stairs. On the sidewalk the detective turned to Mike. "You phoned me earlier," he said. "You have some information?"

"Not exactly," Mike replied. Then he went on to tell what had happened when he and Lori McKay walked into her room the night before. Vincennes listened intently as the tale unfolded; he remained silent for several seconds after Mike had finished. "You have any idea who this person was?"

"None," Mike said.

"Nor the reason for the attempt?"

"No."

"A suggestion? Some suspicion, even?"

"Not even that."

"Do you believe that Miss McKay told the truth when she said she had no idea who might've taken her key?"

"I don't think she has the faintest idea of who... or why."

"I'll ask her."

"Meanwhile," Mike said, "I have to stay around until you solve this thing?"

Vincennes smiled. "I've talked with your firm in New York on the phone. The reports on your character are reassuring. You understand I'm sorry to keep you here, but perhaps it won't be for too long. I hope we'll soon get the break that we need. Meanwhile, you might learn something; remember something that will help us speed up the process to a correct solution."

He smiled again. "It's happened before. I've found that a man involved in some crime will often talk to a fellow suspect more freely than he will to the police. I'd like to think that you'll assist us if possible since it'll be to our mutual advantage."

He offered Mike a handshake, and then nodded to his partner. They stepped toward their waiting brown Ford sedan.

Chapter 13

Mike Barnes thought it over as he got into his own car and drove away. It seemed a little silly to assume that he could be of much help to Vincennes. He had made some inquiries which had accomplished almost nothing, and he realized that his detective skills – compared to those of Captain Vincennes – left a lot to be desired. He thought he could understand the direction in which Vincennes was headed: there seemed ample evidence to suspect Abe Crawford of having the ability and the opportunity to kill Harlow, but the character and motive of the two men who had searched his hotel room and Crawford's apartment seemed the most likely to be involved in Donovan Harlow's death.

Right now, though, his concern was more with Lori McKay's safety than with any more investigation of murder. But before he headed back to the hotel to find her, he wanted to satisfy his desire to know the background of some of the others involved. A chat with Eduardo Espinosa might be beneficial, not that he had any notion that Espinosa was guilty. But as long as he was on this side of town, there was someone else who might talk freely to him if properly approached. Mike pulled the car over to the curb to consult the city map. Fifteen minutes later he stopped in front of a spacious-looking home in a classy-looking neighborhood, behind which the ground fell away into a jungle-like tangle of tall trees, bushes and vines.

When Mike stepped out onto the curb he stood a few moments, struck by the contrast of the street with its expensive homes and groomed lawns and the abruptness of the dense forest bordering them at the rear. It was a sight he would not see in New York.

That impression faded as he considered the elegant house in front of him. Neatly stenciled on the mailbox was the name *Major Orlando Barbary.* An open garage door revealed one empty stall.

Mike pressed the doorbell button. A very casually-dressed Mrs. Barbary pulled open the door. She smiled at him and said rather matter-of-factly, "I was beginning to get a little bored with my own company... please, come in."

Mike stepped inside to a spacious, comfortable-looking living room that ran the full depth of the house, multiple windows giving a wonderful view of the valley and woods.

"Would you like a drink?" Celeste Barbary asked.

"No, thank you," Mike replied. He thought it was much too early for that.

Celeste fluffed the pillows on the sofa and sat down. She patted a spot three feet away from her, inviting Mike to make himself comfortable. This was the first time he had been close to her, and remembering his first impression, he saw nothing to change his mind. Even in shorts and blouse she somehow appeared regal, although the adjective that popped into his head now was more like *snooty.* But beyond all else, she had an attractive figure, and Mike could tell she liked others to admire it. She wasn't strikingly pretty, but still quite attractive with dark hair and hazel eyes. Her face spoke of character and determination, and Mike sensed something about her that was quite intriguing.

His inspection and thought process took only a few seconds, and he gave her his best smile, not knowing what to expect of the situation. But then he remembered he had come for information and quickly decided to omit any social pleasantries, so as not to confuse her with the purpose of his visit.

"I'm a little curious," he said, and before he could continue, Celeste interrupted.

"I suppose you want to know why I was at Donovan's apartment."

"Well, I—"

"The Barbary ménage has reached the point of rupture."

"Because of last night?"

"Oh, no. It's been building up for quite some time." She looked at Mike briefly and then her glance fell to her hands in her lap. Her whole body seemed to droop, and her eyes glazed over with a look of despair. Sitting this close, Mike could see that she was making an obvious effort to control her emotions, apparently unwilling to make any honest display of her real feelings.

"Last night," she went on, her voice low and less assertive, "is... well, I haven't quite accepted it yet. I suppose it's like that with any woman who loses someone she counts on. I know it happened, and it can't be changed. It's just made things harder for me, because now I have to do what I have to do alone. The end result will be about the same, though."

She turned to Mike again. "My husband is probably at the bank right now making sure I don't have access to his money. He knows that if I get my hands on enough I'll leave him, and he intends to make sure I don't."

Her bluntness surprised Mike. But now he could ask a question that he would not have otherwise dared. "Were you in love with Donovan?"

Her expression didn't change much. "I guess so," she said in a dull tone.

"You were going to leave with him on Friday, weren't you?"

"Yes, I was." Her gaze remained fixed on the view of the

116

trees outside the window. Her thoughts were obviously farther away than this room. "He already had the reservations. I just couldn't stand it here any longer."

"Mr. Barbary knew that?"

"Oh, I think he did."

"And he came to Harlow's yesterday afternoon with a gun in his pocket."

"Did he?" she said.

"Could he have gone there last night?"

"I don't know. I've thought about it, and... I just don't know."

"Did he know you were having dinner with Donovan last night?"

"Yes, he knew. I told him so."

"Was he here when you got back?"

"No."

Mike paused, remembering the interviews at Vincennes' office the night before. Waiting for her to elaborate, he didn't want to break her train of thought.

"I'd put the car in the garage and unlocked the door," she continued. "I went into the kitchen for a cold drink when I thought I heard his car. He came in a little after that."

A little excitement stirred Mike's thoughts as he recalled what Major Barbary had told Detective Vincennes. Celeste had been telling her story, and he broke in with: *"It couldn't have been much later because she was home at ten after nine and I don't think she could drive that distance in less than fifteen minutes."*

This was to imply that Barbary knew when his wife came home, and therefore he must have been at home when she arrived. Instead, Celeste had arrived in his absence. "You didn't tell the detective that," Mike said quietly without too much emphasis.

"He didn't ask me."

Mike didn't think that was a very good answer, but he didn't want to pursue the matter any further. He could inform Vincennes of the fact, unless Vincennes already knew the truth.

"What did your husband say when he came in?"

"Oh, he was sarcastic, as usual, pretending it didn't matter. He said he'd been at the country club and he was glad to see I was home early. Then he went into his study and closed the door." She leaned back against the sofa cushions. Her face seemed troubled. Her eyes gazed distantly out the window again, as if she had suffered a temporary defeat.

"Were things different before Donovan Harlow came along?" Mike's curiosity pushed him on.

"Different, maybe, but not good. It's hard to remember when they were good."

"But you married him."

"Yes, I know," she sighed. "We met in Washington. I was working there as a secretary in the administration building. His wife had died the year before and his children were all grown and away. He was polite and considerate, older but good-looking and well-mannered. We started dating, and after a while he asked me to marry him and go with him to Wisconsin and I said yes.

"Maybe it was because things were heating up in the Middle East again, and I thought I wanted to get out of Washington. Or maybe it was because I was twenty-eight years old, and I realized that my dream man hadn't come along yet. I suppose I wasn't in love, but I wanted to be, so I thought I was."

Celeste shifted her weight around and then sat up

straight. "I couldn't have been more wrong," she said. "I soon found out that he was jealous and demanding. He was too old to change, and he told me it was up to me to adapt to his ways, and that his position demanded that we associate with the *right people...* mostly with couples as narrow-minded and self-centered as he was." Now there was a little bitterness in her voice.

"At first I tried to please him. I knew it wasn't working out, but I stuck it out for as long as I could stand it. Finally I told him I wanted a divorce. He said no."

"Because he loves you?"

"Because of his pride. I'd made a promise and I'd damn well better stick to it. According to him I didn't know how well off I was. And of course, he didn't want the humiliation of a divorce and look bad to his friends."

She stopped as if she had finished what she had to say. Mike thought he could understand her discontent, but he found it difficult to feel sorry for her since he knew nothing about her husband's side of the story. Nevertheless he formed an opinion. Here was a passionate woman who wanted attention and maybe a little excitement in her life, and she was, perhaps, a little too volatile except for someone like Donovan Harlow to handle. Recalling his handsome looks and his reckless manner, Mike could appreciate her attraction to him. She definitely had the spirit to challenge her husband for another chance at a better life.

Mike had second thoughts about probing any deeper into her personal affairs, but he had come this far, so he decided to proceed, giving the option to decline. "How did things get started between you and Donovan? Or should I mind my own business and just shove off?"

Celeste gave him a fragile smile and she seemed to find

new interest, as though she was just beginning to notice him as a person. She assessed his open shirt collar and his damp and tousled hair and the gentleness in his eyes. "No, don't go," she said. "I don't mind. I'm glad you're here." She shifted her weight around to find a more comfortable position. "I guess it started at the Royal Palace," she continued. "My husband and I had been out to dinner somewhere else with some friends. We stopped there afterward for drinks. By that time Orlando was upset with me because he thought I had been spending too much time at dinner talking to the young Army captain who was along as someone's guest. Being the jealous sort that he is, Orlando had to put me in my place... turned his back to me and ignored me. Whenever I said anything he was ready with some politely sarcastic remark, and finally I got aggravated.

"I noticed Donovan sitting at the bar having a drink, so I went over and took the stool next to him. I'd met him before – he talks to everyone who comes in his place – knew him well enough to exchange greetings on a first name basis. So I said hello, he smiled and offered to buy me a drink. I accepted, and we talked.

"Somehow I think Donovan knew there was a little trouble between me and Orlando and that I was using him to get even. But I also noticed that he was genuinely interested in me... I could tell. We talked some more, I flirted a little, and he made a few verbal passes that were... well... flattering.

"I think that was the first time in months I'd had a chance to talk to someone who wasn't hung up on social protocol or city politics. I don't know... maybe it was the brandy... but at any rate, I was attracted to him. Anyway, by the time Orlando came and practically hauled me off the stool, we'd made a date to go for a walk through the arboretum and have lunch.

"That was it," she said. "Things just sort of developed, and there came the day when I knew I was in love with him. And it wasn't that I was lured by some illusion. I knew there'd never be a little cottage in the country with a picket fence and dogs and children and flower gardens. I was ready for some adventure, and I was willing to take some chances."

"You knew about Bridget Palmer?"

"Donovan never loved her," Celeste answered quickly.

"But how did Bridget feel about it?"

Celeste shrugged her shoulders. "Don't know. She practically lived with him for over a year."

"Did you know her?"

"Not very well."

"think she hated Donovan enough at the end to kill him?"

She considered the question a few moments and her eyelids closed for a brief while. "She might have... she might have wanted to, but I don't think she'd have the nerve."

"You don't like her."

"That doesn't mean I think she'd kill him. Maybe she did. It could've been some sudden fit of temper. Guess it doesn't take nerve for that to happen. But if you're asking if I think she'd *plan* to kill Donovan... the answer is no."

"What about your husband?"

Celeste stared at Mike with a puzzled expression.

"I mean... if he ever had to stand trial for Donovan's murder, what side would you be on?"

Her eyes opened wide, as if the idea had never had never crossed her mind. "I don't know," she said thoughtfully. "If he killed Donovan..." She paused, and grimaced. "Yes," she said. "I think I would help."

"Even if it meant he went to prison for life?"

"For murder," she said quietly, "he would deserve it."

Chapter 14

Back in his rented car, Mike headed toward the Royal
Palace. He had nearly exhausted all his sources for
information. Reviewing his activities of the past three
and a half hours he found here and there a point of
information that stood out as potential importance in regard
to Donovan Harlow's murder, although nothing could be
substantiated. He had, though, narrowed his field of
speculation.

But there was still nothing to indicate the identity of the
person who had broken into Lori McKay's hotel room with the
intention of killing her.

At this hour the Royal Palace Restaurant was quite busy.
Most of the booths and many of the tables were occupied.
Mike went right to the bar to ask if Eduardo Espinosa had
come in.

"He's here now," the bartender said. "In the kitchen, I
believe."

"What about Bridget Palmer?"

"Over there." The bartender pointed to a table almost
hidden from Mike's sight by the piano. Bridget didn't look up
until he was standing next to her. An empty plate indicated
she had finished her lunch, but there was a full cup of coffee in
front of her.

"Hi," he said. "May I sit down?"

"If you want," Bridget replied without much enthusiasm.

Mike eased into a chair. "Have you made up your mind
yet?"

"About what?"

"You had a proposition, remember? You were going to
clear me with Vincennes... for a price." He watched her take a

sip of coffee.

Bridget's expression drooped, and she was obviously evading his stare. "I said I'd think it over, okay?" she said. "Well, I'm thinking it over."

"And, I suppose," Mike said, "looking for a higher bidder."

"What?"

Mike was clearly irritated with her smugness. "Come on, Bridget, I didn't just crawl out from under a cabbage leaf," he said with sternness in his voice. "Why would you limit yourself to just me when someone else might pay more? Isn't that about it?"

Bridget sipped her coffee. She squirmed in her chair, let out a sigh, and her stare across the room, as if she were bored, seemed an obvious attempt to ignore him.

Mike no longer cared if he was polite or not. "I've been talking to a few people since I saw you," he said. "From what I hear, Abe Crawford has moved into the number one slot since Donovan dumped you."

"What?" Bridget replied. A sudden glare in her eyes told Mike that she clearly understood what he meant.

"You've been seeing Abe Crawford."

"I've been seeing a lot of guys."

"Eduardo Espinosa?"

"Eduardo?" she sneered. "I never see him outside this restaurant."

"But somebody's got some information about the murder. You don't know what it is, but it's for sale, just the same. I guess that makes you some sort of decoy."

She threw down her napkin on the table. "I don't have to sit here and listen to this."

"Why not, Bridget? You wanted to make a deal. Okay. So let's make a deal."

"If at all, when I'm ready."

Mike noticed the kitchen door open. Eduardo Espinosa came out and walked to an empty stool at the bar. Mike pushed back his chair. "All right, Bridget," he said. "Have it your way." He stood up and gave her a sarcastic smile. "Just one suggestion," he added. "Be sure to make up your mind before it's too late."

"Too late for what?"

"To get yourself in the clear."

Mike waited a couple of seconds, both hands on the back of the chair until she gave her full attention. Something that seemed like fear flickered in her eyes. Then she forced an unconvincing laugh. "Thanks for the tip," she said, and reached for her cigarettes.

Eduardo Espinosa sat at the bar, a half-full wine glass in front of him. Looking composed and immaculately neat in his pressed light blue suit, he smiled at Mike in recognition. "I'm about to have lunch. Would you care to join me?"

"No, thank you," Mike responded. "But I'll have a beer. I was here earlier, but you weren't in yet."

"Yes, I was with Captain Vincennes," Eduardo said in his accented tones. "It seems that I am still under some suspicion."

"Is it because of the agreement he found in Harlow's safe?"

"And because Vincennes has learned that Donovan was about to borrow two hundred thousand dollars on this place."

"Then, if Harlow had left town alive, as he planned to do, he would have left you with the business."

"Yes."

"But you'd also be up to your neck in debt."

"Yes."

"But now, you have the business without the debt."

"The captain has reminded me of this repeatedly," Eduardo said.

"Well, it's true, isn't it?"

"Ahh, but if you are suggesting that I could have killed Donovan, I have an alibi." Espinosa took a sip from his wine glass and smiled. "*You* are my alibi."

"Me? How am I your alibi?"

"Let's recall what happened," Eduardo said. "I was here in the restaurant last night, as you know. This young, pretty lady… what is her name?"

"Lori McKay."

"Yes. She comes in, and I tell her that Donovan Harlow is not here. I direct her to the office, and in a few minutes you come to me and ask what she wanted. You go up the stairs to see what has become of her and when you come back down, you seem alarmed. Then you tell me that you will go to the other entrance, and I am still here when you leave. Is that not an alibi?"

"Not any more," Mike replied.

"I beg your pardon?" Eduardo said.

Mike took some time to arrange his thoughts. He had been doing a lot of thinking during the past few hours, and he had recalled certain things that had not occurred to him the night before, but now they were resurfacing in a new light.

"I'm a lawyer," he said.

Espinosa nodded. "Yes, I know."

"Lawyers deal with hypothetical cases all the time. They have to make assumptions. So, let's assume that you had murder on your mind for some time and you were waiting for the right opportunity."

"I do not like that assumption," Eduardo said, "but

continue."

"Your alibi is weak, and here's why. When I came back down those stairs from the office last night and told you I didn't find Miss McKay, you had a menu in your hand – you generally always do when you're working. You said you didn't have a key to the apartment office, but that doesn't have to be the truth. My assumption is that you do have one, and you had plenty of time while I was going around the block to the other door. You could've gone up there from this end."

"Purely speculative," Eduardo responded.

"Maybe," Mike said, his mind processing the event, his tone more aggressive, but very much in control. "But not unsupported. There was a menu in the office... the *apartment* office."

"There was?"

"On the desk. I remember pushing it aside to get to the phone." He leaned forward as to emphasize his next remark. "How did it get there?"

Eduardo took the last gulp from his glass and set it down, patted his lips with a napkin and turned to Mike. His smile seemed a charade. "Is this not your assumption, Mr. Barnes?"

"Yeah," Mike came back promptly. "I say you put it there to have your hands free when you went through the office, and forgot it in your hurry to get out."

"It could have been left there earlier." Eduardo slid off the stool. "According to the young lady's story, the attack on her in the darkness must have happened while I was still here."

"Sure," Mike said. "But whoever jumped her doesn't have to be the killer. Someone else was there. I think I heard him leave, and if you went up there... and I think you did... he probably saw you too."

"And how did this person leave?"

"By the bedroom window. The alley leads right to your kitchen door."

"Yes. It's for delivery of supplies."

"Is it padlocked at night?"

"Certainly." He paused as a waiter came to his side and whispered something in his ear. "You will excuse me, now," he said stiffly. "My lunch is waiting."

"One other thing before you go," Mike said, touching Eduardo's shoulder. "Crawford is hard up, and wants money. I was wondering if he had come to see you this morning."

Eduardo moved his shoulder to avoid Mike's touch. "I have told you... I was with Captain Vincennes all morning," he said and walked away.

Chapter 15

It was after one when Mike returned to the hotel. He went directly to his room on the sixth floor, picked up the phone and dialed room 306. When Lori McKay did not answer, he rode the elevator back to the atrium main floor and began a search. He soon found her sitting at a table with two other people. One was a young man about his own age, tall and thin, wearing a plaid sport shirt, wire-rimmed glasses, and looked as though he might be rather awkward. The other was a smartly-dressed woman, perhaps in her fifties. Deciding that these were the traveling mates Lori had spoken of, and who he had seen just briefly through an open doorway, he was too close now to detour without appearing rude. He smiled at them, said hello, and came reluctantly to a stop.

Lori's reaction was pleasant enough but hardly enthusiastic. She introduced her table companions as Mrs. Flagstone and her nephew, Daniel. Daniel clumsily unfolded his six feet and some inches, stood, and shook hands with Mike. "Won't you sit down?" he said.

"Just for a minute," Mike replied, noting that they had not quite finished their lunch. He wanted to talk to Lori, but he knew he wouldn't have a chance now because Mrs. Flagstone was demanding his attention.

Aristocratic-looking, Mrs. Flagstone was attractive and her mostly gray hair was quite becoming to her. Her intense, vivacious manner bubbled as she said she had hoped to meet him. "Lori has been telling us about you and what happened last night," she said. "Have the police determined who did it yet?"

"I don't think so," Mike said.

Mrs. Flagstone turned to Lori. "Just imagine," she said.

"Coming all the way up here and then practically tripping over a murder. It's the most exciting thing I ever heard of." Then she turned back to Mike. "Will you have to stay here until they have completed the investigation?"

"I'm not sure how long I'll have to stay," Mike said. And then Mrs. Flagstone rambled on with more questions and he found he could answer without much concentration simply by nodding with a yes or no every now and then while she supplied all the energy and vocalizing. Meanwhile he was relieved to see that Lori displayed no open hostility toward him. When he had the chance he asked if Vincennes had seen her.

"Yes," she said.

"Vincennes?" Mrs. Flagstone interrupted with new interest.

"He's the homicide investigator," Mike informed her.

"Really!" She looked at Lori. "He came to see you this morning? Oh, I wish I could have met him. What's he like?"

Lori gave a brief, unflattering characterization.

"What did he have to say?" Mike asked.

"He just asked me a few questions."

"About what, dear?" Mrs. Flagstone said. "Certainly he doesn't suspect you, does he?"

The conversation had become too one-sided to suit Mike. He pushed back his chair. It seemed that Lori had not yet mentioned the incident in her room to Mrs. Flagstone, and he wanted to get away before he became involved in that.

"I wish you wouldn't go," Mrs. Flagstone said. "We'll see you later, won't we?"

Mike lied politely. "I hope so." Then he turned to Lori again. "I'll call you," he said. "Maybe we can go for that swim."

Lori shrugged her shoulders. "I don't know... I'm not

really in the mood for that now."

Unable to counter the rejection, Mike just walked away. He continued on until he reached the lounge across the atrium where he found a small table that afforded him some privacy. He ordered a sandwich and a beer, and consumed them without delay. Right now he was brooding, and he understood the source of his unhappiness. He was determined to do something about it at his first opportunity.

He went to his room, took off his shirt and flopped down on the bed. The lack of sleep was taking its toll. He was exhausted. He closed his eyes, and in a short time he was asleep.

Chapter 16

I t seemed like he had only dozed off for a few minutes, but when Mike opened his eyes and glanced at his watch it was after three. He sat up, dry-mouthed, a little groggy, and his scalp felt damp. He summoned his energy to walk over to the windows and gazed out at a cloudy sky. Going for a swim would do him good, he thought, if he could find the energy to make the effort. Instead, he sat down in the chair, lit a cigarette, and considered any other options.

His first decision was simple: he had done all the chasing around he was going to do. For all he knew, Vincennes had the case all wrapped up by now, and in any event there was nothing more that he could accomplish in the matter of Donovan Harlow's murder. He stuck to that decision for, perhaps, five seconds, until he remembered that Scott Newman at the *State Journal* was supposed to be getting him some information. Finding Newman and treating him to a few brews at his favorite beer garden would be the thing to do, but the time of day was wrong – Newman would be at work during a busy time.

But perhaps he could go into town and poke around. Perhaps not. He decided there wasn't much he really wanted to do in town. Then it dawned on him what he *should be doing*. He wanted most to see Lori McKay. Being with her made him feel good. He wanted to explain about Bridget Palmer, and once he had done that everything would be all right, because he thought Lori was the type who would accept an honest explanation. He picked up the phone and dialed room 306, but there was only a busy signal.

Mike headed into the bathroom. There was no need to feel disappointed, as he knew Lori was in her room. He brushed his teeth, slapped cold water on his face, and combed his hair. When he went back to the phone, Lori answered.

"Hello, Miss McKay," he said. "This is Mike Barnes. How about going for a swim now?"

"I'm sorry."

"Still not in the mood?"

"I have to go into town in about a half an hour."

"Oh," Mike said, his disappointment coming out. "Well, how about dinner?"

"I... I'm not sure how long I'll be. You'd better not plan on it."

"Well, then, would you mind if I called you later?"

"No, I wouldn't mind at all."

After Mike had hung up the phone, be swore at himself. Now, suddenly he understood his problem. Until now, he had been thinking only of himself. Because he wanted so much to be with her, some foolish sensitivity, an occupational hazard for a man in love, had obscured the one important issue. Someone had tried to kill her, and they might have been successful had he not been with her the previous night. He had promised himself earlier that he would stay with her until he knew she was safe, and now he felt like a jerk for not mentioning that to her. But he knew where she was and where she was going. It would be easy enough to intercept her at the front entrance.

He dressed hurriedly but with some care, checking his pockets for money and keys before he left the room. No more than a few minutes had elapsed when he reached his rental car in the parking lot and drove it under the canopy at the main entrance. He waited there a little while, then got out and took up a position where he could keep an eye on the revolving doors.

Lori McKay appeared about five minutes later. She didn't see Mike right away as she peered out across the drive in search for an approaching taxi. He stepped up beside her and nudged her arm before she was aware of him. It startled her a little. "Oh," she said, and her green eyes widened as she glanced his way.

"I was going down town, too," Mike said. "So I thought I could give you a lift."

"But I called a cab."

"You can call and cancel it. I really wanted to talk to you anyway." He took her arm and began walking, guiding her toward his car.

Lori drew a deep breath and sighed, reluctantly following his lead.

"First of all, I want to tell you about Bridget." He opened the passenger door and Lori sat down. As Mike closed the door again, he noticed a little smile curl on the corners of her mouth. "Actually," she said as Mike got in behind the wheel. "I've been dying to hear about Bridget. I guess I acted sort of foolish this morning."

"No, you didn't. It could be expected."

"I was just so surprised. I must've looked pretty funny stalking off the way I did. What was it she said? 'Come in, honey. I was just leaving?'"

Mike laughed. "Yeah, I was surprised, too. I thought it was you when she knocked. I'd just gotten up, and I expected to see you when I opened the door, but instead, there stood Bridget."

"She didn't phone first?"

"No."

"Well, what did she want?"

"She had a proposition," Mike went on, the laughter gone

now. He explained about the conversation they'd had and the scheme that Bridget had proposed. By the time he had finished, the lighthearted mood in both had diminished, and their thoughts were cast backward to death and murder.

"What does it all mean?" Lori asked. "That's blackmail, isn't it?"

"It would be if I paid her."

"Do you think she knows who killed Donovan Harlow?"

"I doubt it." Mike hesitated while he sorted his thoughts into logical order. "I'd guess that someone sent her."

"But, why?"

"To see what the chances were of collecting."

"Have you seen her since?"

"I saw her at the Royal Palace," Mike said. "I was looking for Eduardo and she was having lunch. I asked if she was ready to make a deal, but she just stalled... didn't want to talk about it... acted like she just wanted to get rid of me."

"Have any idea who sent her?"

"I'm guessing that it was Abe Crawford."

"Oh." Lori's tone sounded strange. "Why do you say that?"

Mike glanced at her. She was just staring down at her hands in her lap and she seemed oddly pale.

"I talked to a few people this morning," Mike explained. "Seems that Abe Crawford has become the number-one boyfriend since she broke up with Donovan. And it also seems that Abe needs money and... I don't know... it just figures."

"Are you going to tell the detectives about Bridget?"

"Probably," he said, looking back at the heavy afternoon traffic on University Avenue. He realized that there were several things he should tell Detective Vincennes. "Where downtown are you going?" When she didn't reply he asked, "Shopping?"

Lori shook her head. "No," she said in a tone Mike could barely hear. "I was going to see Mr. Crawford."

Mike thought he had heard her clearly enough, but he was having difficulty accepting her statement. "Crawford? Did you say Crawford?"

"He called me... a little while before you did... said he couldn't talk on the phone, and he couldn't leave his place because he was expecting another important call. He said it was important, and that it would only take a few minutes."

"Crawford," Mike said again, his surprise now turning to a little anger backed up by fear. "You were going to see him at his place just because he asked you to?"

"He said it was important and I thought—"

"Have you forgotten what happened in your hotel room last night?"

"Of course not."

"Or maybe you don't care that your life might be in danger."

"Of course I care," she replied with some new-found spirit. "But nobody would try anything like that in broad daylight."

"It won't be broad daylight in Crawford's apartment." He pulled the car into a strip mall parking lot and dug out his map. "Think about it. I just told you that he's the one who probably sent Bridget to see me. He probably knows plenty, and he could even be the one who—"

"But I didn't know that when he called me."

Mike realized that Lori could not have known, and that his anger should not be directed at her. He reached for her hand and gently squeezed it. "I'm sorry," he said smiling. "I didn't mean to snap at you."

"It's okay. If I'd known about all this, I wouldn't have agreed to come." She stared at Mike studying the map. "I have his address."

"Oh, I know where he lives. I've already been there. I'm just looking to see how to get there from here."

"I don't know why I agreed to come in the first place." Lori seemed annoyed with herself. "But he was so insistent..."

"Maybe it will turn out to be a good idea," Mike assured her. "We'll both go to see Mr. Crawford."

"Do you think we should? I mean..."

"Why not? He's got some important information for you." He grinned to indicate a level of confidence. "I'm just tagging along as your attorney."

Lori remained silent after that, but obviously a little uneasy. A few minutes later Mike eased the car up to the curb opposite Crawford's apartment building, somewhat closer than he had done that morning. They crossed the street and Mike took Lori's arm as they went up the steps into the entry. There was no need to look at the card tacked to the door this time as he knocked. There was no answer so he knocked again. Still no answer. He knocked again, louder this time, and when there was no response from inside, Mike tried the knob. The door opened, just as before. He called out, "Anybody home? Hey, Crawford!"

No one answered, and at first Mike didn't suspect anything to be wrong. Crawford had telephoned Lori, the door was unlocked, and so Abe must be there, perhaps in another room where he didn't hear. Mike took another step forward and was about to call out again when he stopped, the tension instantly tying his stomach in a knot.

His scan of the dim, quiet room had moved to the area just

behind the cluttered coffee table. With only the light from the curtained front windows, he saw first the upturned shoes and trouser legs. He had to take a sideways step to see the rest of the shadowed figure that lay awkward and still beside an overturned chair. Aware of Abe Crawford's fondness of whiskey, and knowing that he had started drinking earlier that morning, it didn't seem at all surprising that he had fallen in a drunken stupor. He might have just been passed out, but there seemed some strange and unnatural limpness had taken over. Mike's glance moved swiftly across Crawford's wrinkled slacks and the loud sport shirt, searching for some obvious, incapacitating injury. Only when he focused on the blond, curly head did he see the dark trickle behind one ear.

Now he understood why Crawford had not answered his call, and without leaning closer he knew that Abe would never answer again.

A sound behind him reminded him of Lori, and he stepped back, swallowing against a rising nausea. She was still standing just inside the threshold, the door still open behind her. He stepped past her to close the door as she said, "What is it?" Leading her to the sliding glass door onto a patio, he opened it and told her to stay there.

Back in the center of the room once more he kneeled beside the body. In search for a pulse that never came, without meaning to, his mind went back to the night before when he had held another lifeless hand that seemed as warm as his own. The surroundings were different, but the pattern was the same except that Donovan Harlow had taken a bullet in the chest. Without realizing it, Mike's glance moved in a widening circle in search of a gun.

It was then that he heard the short metallic sound that broke the silence, but he thought Lori must have made it and paid no attention. Not until he heard it a second time did he glance up, and even then his first reaction was one of disbelief. It didn't seem possible that the pattern of murder could be so exactly repeated that he should hear the same sounds here that he had heard the night before. No, it couldn't be.

The sounds he had heard then had come from the opening or closing of the metal grill protecting Harlow's bedroom window, and he was quite certain that Abe Crawford had made it when he escaped through the window into the alley. This sound seemed heavier and more solid, like a door being closed, not in this room but somewhere else.

To make sure, he turned to Lori. "Was that you?"

She shook her head, her eyes wide and her face ghostly pale. "No," she said, "but I heard it. It's Mr. Crawford, isn't it?" she whispered. "He's dead, isn't he?"

Mike was back on his feet, his gaze focused on the doorway of the room beyond. He ignored Lori's plea not to go there, and with his scalp tingling he reached around the corner and found a light switch.

The bedroom was empty, and there were no signs of a struggle. Everything seemed to be in place, as if no search had been made. The adjoining bath was rather untidy, and Mike didn't linger there.

He went through the French doors into the kitchen and dining area. Windows overlooked a back patio, and before he touched the door, he covered his hand with his handkerchief. He opened and closed the door several times quietly, experimenting and listening to the sounds it made, confident that he knew this was the origin of the sounds he had heard. When he stepped out onto the patio, he saw a fence encompassing the back yard, and a gate swung open to the deserted alley. As he stood there, a car engine started

138

somewhere nearby, but its sound was soon masked by the noise of a city bus accelerating up the next street.

Mike stayed there a few moments in silence. Even though he was quite certain that the perpetrator was gone, he felt the pressure of fear, not for himself but for Lori. The hair on the back of his neck bristled. Last night someone had stolen her room key and waited in the darkness with a gun. Now it seemed that someone had waited here, too, left the front door unlocked, just to get another chance at her. It was possible that Crawford had made the call to Lori McKay, although it may have been at gunpoint. And it might not have been him who called at all, as Lori would not have recognized his voice.

The killer might have been surprised by their arrival. But it seemed more likely that this someone had waited here on purpose, knowing that Lori would show up because of the phone call. All these thoughts formulated in Mike's head in just a few seconds, and apart from his fears one fact stood out above the rest. "Dear God," he whispered as he turned back toward the kitchen. He gave silent thanks for the impulse that had made him wait for Lori at the hotel. Luck or coincidence, whatever it was that shaped his actions at the right time, had functioned just the way it should have. It brought him here with her, and for this he was grateful.

Chapter 17

Lori had remained standing by the patio door. Mike walked to her, took her arm and guided her to an easy chair. "You should sit down," he said.

"Shouldn't we call the police?" She sank down into the chair without protest.

"Yes," Mike replied, and then he remembered that he had intended to call Scott Newman, as well.

He understood that he should not disturb the body before the police arrived, but prompted by some ideas that had begun to mushroom in his mind, he felt the need to satisfy a few questions. First he checked the pockets of Abe's shirt, finding in one a pack of cigarettes, and in the other, his pilot credentials and passport in a black leather case. Then, the trousers pockets contained some loose change and keys. They were insignificant so he put them back and reached under the body to slip a wallet out of the hip pocket. There he found a few dollars in bills, a driver's license, several business cards, and finally a small slip of paper that caught and held his interest. Penciled on the paper were the notations:

R-22 L-13 R-9 L-37 R-2 L-17

Mike guessed that it was a combination, probably for Donovan Harlow's safe. Certain that there was nothing else of interest in the wallet, he returned the cards and paper and slipped it back into the pocket. He was still knelt on one knee when an unexpected knock on the door shattered the stillness.

Every muscle in his body tensed as he came to his feet, a finger to his lips signaling Lori to remain silent. She was already standing, and together they tiptoed to the bedroom. Just as he snapped off the light he heard the door open. He couldn't see who entered, but he soon recognized the voice.

"Abe?" Bridget Palmer called out. "Where are you, honey?"

The door closed, and there were a few moments of silence. Then came the anguished, horrified cry, followed by the pounding of feet across the floor. Bridget was on her knees, shaking Crawford's shoulder and moaning his name. Her blond hair had fallen forward, hiding her face.

Mike came out of the bedroom with Lori just a step behind. When he touched Bridget's shoulder she gave a shocking and terrified scream and scrambled crab-like to one side.

"Bridget!" Mike said.

She looked up and flung her hair back. Her eyes were wild, like those of a cornered animal. "You did it!" she screeched.

"No... Listen," Mike said to her, not sure that she even recognized him. He grabbed her shoulder and shook it. "Take it easy," he said harshly, thinking bluntness would be more effective than sympathy. "If we're going to find out who did this, you've got to help."

"But he was all right just a few minutes ago," she cried.

He helped her to her feet. "Then tell us about it," he said, and held her when she started swaying. With Lori's help they got her to a chair, and she buried her face in her hands, sobbing and rocking back and forth. Instead of trying to stop her, Mike went to the kitchen, found a bottle of whisky in a cabinet, and poured some into a glass.

"Here," he said when he returned to the crying woman.

Bridget looked up at him. "I don't want it."

He set the glass on the table. "All right," he said bending over her. "Now what do you mean, he was all right a few minutes ago?"

"I... I just talked to him on the phone," she replied, her voice cold and empty.

"When?"

"Twenty minutes... maybe a half-hour ago."

"What did he say?"

"He asked if I could come over."

"Are you sure it was him on the phone?"

Bridget gave Mike an odd stare. "Of course it was him."

"Do you have any idea who might've done this?"

"No."

"But he knew who killed Harlow, didn't he?"

She looked at him again blankly and he shook her shoulder again, hating his callousness but knowing it was necessary. "Didn't he?" he repeated.

"I... I don't know."

"But you've got some idea. He sent you to my hotel room this morning, didn't he? Who else was he trying to blackmail?"

"I told you. I don't know."

Mike took a deep breath and considered the information as he knew it. Crawford had not killed Harlow. That much seemed obvious now. But he had been there; otherwise he could not have known who was involved. Most likely he was there when Mike discovered the body, and had been searching the place when Lori knocked at the office door. But Crawford had not been in the Royal Palace, so he must have entered the apartment some other way.

"You were Donovan's girlfriend for some time," Mike said to Bridget. "Did you have a key to his apartment?"

"Donovan gave it to me. I never gave it back. He never asked for it."

"So you gave it to Crawford... didn't you?"

"Yes."

"Why?"

"Because he asked for it... yesterday."

"You knew the combination to his safe, too, didn't you?"

Bridget's eyes narrowed, but she didn't answer.

"He has a combination written down in his wallet," Mike said. "Where else would he get it? You must've given it to him. How did you get it?"

"I used to watch Donovan," she finally said. "It was like a game. I got one number, then another. It took me a long time, but I never used it," she said defensively. "I never thought of it until... " Her voice trailed off, her expression full of stress.

Lori touched Mike's arm. He glanced at her and saw her wet, concerned eyes. She nodded toward Bridget. "Do you have to, Mike?" she asked softly. "I mean, couldn't it wait?"

He shook his head and returned his stare at Bridget. "Look, Bridget," he said sternly. "It's much too late to lie. If you want to help, tell the truth. Were you going away with Crawford after he'd cleaned out the safe?"

"I never had enough money to get out of here on my own," she explained. "I couldn't save anything on my salary. At first I thought Donovan would..." The statement dangled. She sobbed softly and then tried again. "Donovan cheated Abe, just like he cheated me and everyone else. When Abe found out Donovan was getting ready to run out, he was afraid he wouldn't get his share of the plane money."

"The plane they sold in South America?"

"Yes."

Mike understood how the transaction was to be made. That was quite clear. What he didn't know was what had happened to the money.

"You're sure Abe didn't collect in Columbia."

"No. The money was deposited with someone here... some lawyer."

"Do you know the lawyer's name?"

"Not his full name... Donovan just called him John, or Juan, or something like that."

Juan, Mike thought, and supplied the whole name: "Juan Delsoto... the money was to be paid to this lawyer when delivery was confirmed?"

"Yes. But yesterday when Abe went to get his share Donovan told him he hadn't heard from this lawyer."

"Yeah, I know that part, Bridget. I was there and heard that much."

"Anyway, Abe thought he was stalling. He said the only chance to get even, the only chance for us, was to open the safe and take what was his. So I gave him the combination and—"

"And he went up there last night," Mike cut in. "But he didn't need the combination. By that time I think the safe had been knocked open, so he started to search the office. And then Lori knocked. He wasn't about to give up yet, so he grabbed the spread from Harlow's bed, turned off the light and opened the door, ready for anything. If it had been a man he would've just slugged him and he would've had a struggle. But when Lori came in, it was easy."

Mike paused to gather his thoughts, and then continued. "He didn't find any diamonds or cash, and he even missed the nine thousand dollars that Vincennes found later. He must have been there when the shots were fired, and still there when I came in. Then today he saw another chance to collect your getaway money – blackmail... because of what he knew about the murder."

Mike gave some thought to the probability that Abe *had* gotten his share of the plane money, and Julio Martinez had taken it away from him during the visit here this morning. It fit the scenario, too, and the idea would remain Mike's second choice.

He saw Bridget put her head down and he knew he would get no further information from her. From his inside jacket pocket he pulled out the paper with Scott Newman's phone number and his cell phone. He punched in the numbers and was pleasantly surprised not only to hear Scott's voice answer, but to get the information he had asked for.

"Just remember," Newman said, "what I told you about this being confidential. I promised my friend at the bank it would never come back to him. He owed me some favors, and that's the only reason I got it. If you quote me on this, I'll just have to get another friend to break your kneecaps... as a favor, of course," Newman chuckled.

"Okay."

"Two withdrawals—"

"Two?"

"Yeah, but by the same guy. Five thousand from a checking account that nearly wiped it out, and another five thousand from savings..."

Mike listened to the rest of it as his mind raced and certain things started to fall into place. "Okay, Scott. Now, here's something for you." He told the newspaper man briefly about what had happened to Abe Crawford. "Call Captain Vincennes," he said before Newman could interrupt. "Maybe he'll give you an exclusive. Time is important right now, so I can't talk. Tell Vincennes I'll get in touch with him as soon as I can." He hung up quickly because he had no time for explanations. A few seconds later he was talking to the bartender at the Royal Palace. He was told that Espinosa was not in.

"How long ago did he leave . . . a half-hour? Okay, thanks."

Bridget was watching him when he put away his phone. Her expression seemed numb and her brown eyes dull. He knew what he had to do. He went to the back door and locked it. Then he examined the chain lock on the front door and explained to Bridget that the police would be there soon. "You'll have to tell them what happened."

Bridget nodded that she understood.

"Now remember," Mike said. "Abe Crawford was killed for what he knew. You're his girlfriend. If the killer thinks Crawford may have told you too much, you could be next on the list."

"Mike!" Lori exclaimed, her voice sharp with disapproval.

"Well, it's true... make sure you hook this chain when we leave," he said to Bridget. "And make damn sure it's the police before you let anyone in."

"I can wait with her," Lori offered.

"She'll be all right."

"But—"

Mike cut her off because his fear still lingered. Whoever killed Abe Crawford still had a gun, and Lori was apt to be his next target. He did not tell her this, nor did he tell her that he planned to stay with her every minute from now on... no matter what happened. He simply said, "I wish you would just come with me... please."

For another few moments while Mike opened the door and peered up and down the street, she hesitated, troubled as she glanced at Bridget. Then, as if she understood the urgency in Mike's request, she followed him without further argument.

Chapter 18

Captain Quinten Vincennes had been patiently waiting all day for the coded message from the Drug Enforcement Agency. He had been alerted earlier that multiple arrests would occur that day, all simultaneously if their master plan was not interrupted. Vincennes and his department knew very little about the plan. The long term D.E.A. investigation had recently involved only some state and county officials; fewer people privy to the operation blueprint meant less chance of failure due to an information leak. An attempt to flee by one or more of the subjects was the only reason the city police would become directly involved.

D.E.A. undercover agent Fox Bishop had learned of a cocaine dealer, known only as John, operating in the Madison area. Subsequent investigation revealed that John wasn't operating alone, but tracking down the ring of which he was a part had not come easy. Its members were quite elusive. With the help of a trusted informant, Fox managed a few purchases of the white powder from John over a period of several months. Tests made on the drug confirmed that it was the real thing and of high quality.

And now the day had come when, after nearly two years of cat and mouse, Fox was about to tighten the noose on his prime subject known as John, or rather, Julio Martinez. Plans had been carefully laid for Fox's informant to take delivery of a kilo – 2.2 pounds of pure cocaine. The selling price was set at $19,500. But the one big difference this time was that Fox would be in the shadows to witness the transaction, and he would even record the act with a small, inconspicuous, but highly effective video camera.

"He told me to pick up the stuff at the truck shop parking

lot tonight," the informant said on the phone.

"What time?" Fox asked.

"Six-thirty."

"Was he specific about where in the parking lot?"

"Yeah... his car will be parked next to the dumpster on the west side of the shop. I'm supposed to meet him there."

"Did he say what kind of car?"

"Yeah. A maroon Oldsmobile Delta 88."

"Okay, Tony," Fox said, and paused briefly. "Are you up to this? I mean... if he should get nervous about anything... if anything goes wrong... it could get ugly."

"Yeah, I know."

"So, are you still with me?"

"Sure. I can handle it."

"Okay. The cash will be delivered to you by five. Don't try to contact me any more today. Once you have the money, you're on your own. Okay?"

"Okay."

Fox had no choice but to trust Tony. He had been imported to Madison from across the state, so no one knew him here. He'd worked out well with the other buys, and there was no reason to think he wouldn't perform flawlessly this time, just as before.

Fox would be at the truck stop two or three hours before the transaction was to take place, to find his best vantage point. Several back-ups would be there, too, but none of them would arrive together. Every precaution had been taken to insure that Julio or any accomplices would have no reason to be suspicious.

By 4:00 pm Fox had found his best position, his average-looking black Chevy Suburban parked between two trucks, across a traffic lane from the dumpsters, with a clear line of sight to where Julio would be conducting business with Tony. From the profile he had built on Julio Martinez, he knew that four o'clock was the usual starting time for Julio's shift as a mechanic in the truck shop, but tardiness seemed to be the norm.

Fox noticed three of his back-ups roaming the area, looking very much the part of truck drivers, staying casually on the move as not to draw any attention. The stage was set, waiting for its players to make an entrance. Fox was ready to do some business of his own.

Chapter 19

G oing to Juan Delsoto's office again could be a mistake. Mike knew that. But he was also keenly aware that time might be the most important element now, and he went there only because he wanted to make one more attempt at finding out what had happened to the money paid for the DC-3. There was a lot of traffic at this time of day, but the sidewalk was practically deserted when Mike parked at the curb in front of the old brick building. Trusting no one but himself now, as he opened the door he motioned for Lori to get out, saying only that she had better come with him. She made no protest other than to ask where they were going.

"To see a lawyer," Mike said. "A guy named Juan Delsoto. We'll only be a few minutes."

The outer office in the Delsoto suite was empty when Mike opened the door. The typewriter was covered and everything seemed to be neatly put away, the girl apparently gone for the day. Mike continued to the connecting door and knocked. When there was no answer after about five seconds, he turned the knob and pushed the door open, stepped inside, and glanced about the room before allowing Lori to enter.

Delsoto sat behind his desk, a dark, formidable figure, unmoving in his chair except for the black eyes that examined his visitors. He was in shirt sleeves as before, but he no longer appeared relaxed and debonair. He leaned on his forearms, hands clasped on the desktop, and he made no movement as Mike approached. His black hair, so sleekly combed that morning was somewhat mussed now, and Mike noticed a film of nervous perspiration on his dark face.

Because time was so important, Mike didn't waste any words. Without any preliminary greetings he explained what had happened to Crawford. He waited and watched for some reaction, but Delsoto's face remained a brown mask.

After a long pause the lawyer grunted and cleared his throat. "And why do you come to me?"

"I want to know what happened to the money that was paid for the plane Crawford delivered to Columbia."

"I don't have it."

"You were Harlow's lawyer."

"In some things."

"In this deal... according to Crawford," Mike said stretching the truth a little, his voice showing a level of irritation. "The money was paid to you to be turned over when delivery was confirmed."

"I do not have the money," Delsoto insisted. His gaze remained steady, reflecting an attitude that seemed more resentful than defiant. Beads of perspiration still glistened on his face, and he continued to sit motionless as Mike waited while the seconds ticked away.

Finally, Mike's impatience drove him to take some form of action. He could suppress his frustration no longer. He stepped forward and reached for the phone on Delsoto's desk. "Okay," he said abruptly. "If you don't want to tell me about it, maybe you'd rather tell the police." He picked up the receiver, hopeful that his memory could recall Vincennes' number, and half expecting Delsoto to put up some sort of protest. But before he could start dialing Vincennes' number, he heard a startled gasp that he knew came from Lori. He turned to look at her, and then he heard another voice.

"Put the phone down, please!"

It was the protest Mike was expecting, but it wasn't Delsoto's voice. Lori's eyes were fixed on a location across the room. Mike turned, the phone still in his hand. A door opposite the reception office stood open. He had seen it before, assuming it led to an adjoining office, but now he saw that it was a closet-like storage room, and he realized why there was sweat on Delsoto's face.

Moving cautiously forward from the open doorway was the familiar face of Carmen Rios, the man who had accompanied Julio Martinez every time Mike had seen him. But now it appeared that Carmen was alone, and he held in his hand the familiar short-barreled revolver. He stepped across the room to the reception office door, and leaning against it, he folded his arms across his chest but with the gun still in readiness. "You will not need the telephone," he said calmly.

Mike let out his breath slowly. He glanced at Lori. She was watching the man with the gun, startled, but she didn't appear afraid.

"I guess you're right," he said. He put the receiver back, and then stepped over to stand beside Lori.

"I was discussing certain matters of business with Señor Delsoto when we heard your knock," the gunman said. "It seemed better to be out of sight."

"You've been busy boys the last couple of days," Mike said.

"Unfortunately, yes."

"You knocked open Harlow's safe, searched me and my room, and slugged Abe Crawford this morning after you'd searched his place. Now you finally caught up with Delsoto, eh?"

"It took much time to get the necessary information," Carmen said in his polite and quiet way. "But I can tell you that Señor Delsoto spoke the truth."

"When?"

"Just now. He does not have the bank draft." He took a folded yellow check from his pocket. "As you see, I have it now." His eyes darted from Mike to Delsoto and back to Mike as he caught himself in a self-righteous grin. "A few more minutes and I would not have had to trouble you."

"You heard what I said about Abe Crawford?"

Carmen shrugged. "Yes, it is most unfortunate about Señor Crawford."

"You don't know anything about it?"

"No."

"Of course not," Mike said with sarcasm. "You wouldn't kill him just because he sold the plane that was carrying your cargo."

Carmen glanced at his watch. "I do not have much time," he said. "But I suppose you deserve some explanation. My amigo – Julio – and I are not concerned with murder. Señor Harlow and Señor Crawford have carried cargo for us before. This time they were to pick up a shipment—"

"Of guns," Mike cut in. "Or do you call it agricultural tools?"

"Suppose we say equipment."

"From Texas."

Carmen refused to be needled. He remained patient and polite. "From a point in your country to Panama," he said. "The plane left here Sunday to pick up this equipment early Monday morning. We had word that this was done."

"You came to the Royal Palace to see Harlow that night."

"That is so, because we had not yet received word that the cargo had been delivered. When we inquired about the delay, Señor Harlow explained that there may have been some minor breakdown. We accepted that until the following morning when we learned that the pilot – Señor Crawford – had already returned on Tuesday night. We then made other inquiries elsewhere and learned that Crawford had been to

South America, and that he had returned without the plane."

He raised his left arm from the elbow and turned his palm upward. "I know there are certain people in Columbia who would be interested to buy our equipment. And I understand that such a plane as Señor Harlow's would be quite valuable, although I cannot be absolutely certain about such details."

"Your equipment was missing," Mike said, "and you couldn't go to the police because it was contraband."

Carmen shrugged. "Let's say it was something we would rather not discuss with the authorities."

"So you went to Harlow instead. What did he say?"

"He admitted that the plane had been sold, but he insisted that the cargo had been delivered first, as scheduled. We didn't believe this, but it didn't seem wise to use threats. As you can see, this was a difficult situation for us. We had lost our equipment and the money that paid for it. We knew a sale of this kind in Columbia would not be paid in advance, but rather to a third party. But we didn't know who that third party would be, so we decided to see if Harlow had something of equal value to replace our loss."

"Like diamonds."

"We had heard of them."

"So you busted open Harlow's safe Wednesday afternoon after I left the apartment and you knew he was gone. When you didn't find them, or the money, you came to my hotel."

"We did not have great hope, but we knew you had come from New York to see Señor Harlow. It was a possibility we had to explore."

"Okay. So then this morning you went to Crawford still hoping to find the money or a bank draft. Now you've got it. How much is it?"

"Three hundred thousand dollars, American," Carmen

replied. "Fifty thousand for our gu—equipment, and the balance I assume is for the plane."

Mike glanced over at Delsoto as a new thought came to him. The lawyer had finally moved; he was leaning back in his chair, but he sat very still. "How come you didn't pay Harlow?" he asked.

"There was a delay in the acknowledgment," Delsoto said.

"Crawford delivered the plane on Tuesday."

"The wire did not arrive until Wednesday."

"Did Donovan believe that?"

"He had to... it was the truth."

"When did it arrive Wednesday?"

"Not until late in the afternoon. It was too late to go to the bank."

"The draft was in your name?"

Delsoto cleared his throat and took time to glare at Carmen and the weapon before he spoke. "I will say, now, that I had nothing to do with the sale of the plane or its cargo. A gentleman from Columbia came here last week. I had dealt with him before. He had this draft for three hundred thousand dollars. He explained that the party he represented was interested in buying the plane from Harlow and Crawford. He said that I was to hold the draft until he gave word that the transaction had been completed. At that time I was to cash it and give the proceeds to Donovan Harlow, less my fee."

"And I suppose," Mike said, "with Harlow out of the way you intended to hang on to that draft until you could just cash it yourself. Or were you going to give Crawford his share?"

Delsoto tightened his lips and said nothing. Mike turned to Carmen. "The check is in Delsoto's name. What good is it to you?"

"It will be safe with me. Señor Delsoto knows where to reach me. When he delivers my fifty thousand dollars, I will be happy to return the draft to him."

Carmen looked at his watch. "And now," he said, his voice very business-like, "I'm afraid that I must ask your cooperation."

"Our cooperation?" Mike said. "For what?"

"There is a private plane waiting for me at the airport. But in the meantime, the three of you present a problem. If I leave you here, you will inform the police and prevent my departure." He wrinkled his brow. "It would be a simple matter to just lock you up someplace, so, I think it will be best to take a ride in the country."

"So, what are you going to do? Kill us all?"

"Oh! But Señor! Certainly not. I know a place in the country where I can make sure you are confined at least long enough for me to return to the airport. You will be in no danger there. Now, if you will all be so kind as to give me your cell phones." He reminded them that he was armed by waving the revolver for all to see.

Mike understood the situation. He reached in his pocket, pulled out his cell phone and handed it to Carmen, nodding to Lori to do the same. She complied without protest. Delsoto stood, put on his sport jacket, and handed over his cell.

"Okay," the gunman said. "We can all fit in my car. Señor Delsoto will drive. It is just downstairs in front of the door. I will follow you down. If we are sensible about this there is no reason for anyone to get hurt." He put the gun in his pocket but his hand remained on it, the muzzle bulging the fabric in a threatening manner. "We will go now."

Delsoto walked to the door, pulled it open, and stepped into the reception office. Mike took Lori's hand and they moved up behind him. His mind smoldered with the bitter thought of how a blundering impulse had brought them here.

Mike understood Carmen's problem. He believed him when he said there would be no danger if they behaved themselves. Carmen needed to get out of the country and he had a plan for doing just that, and for some unknown reason, Mike didn't resent the attempt. But he was still disgusted with himself for his bad judgment in coming here at all when he realized that time might be the important factor in solving two murders.

He had an idea who had committed them. But in two hours the proof to substantiate that idea might be lost. Instead of focusing on his main objective, he had stopped here only to talk to Delsoto one more time, thinking that it would only take a few minutes. Now his chances were slipping away.

His wandering mind returned to the present situation when he felt Lori's arm move tensely against his grip. "Relax," he said, wanting to reassure her. "If we have to take a ride, we have to take a ride."

"Sure," Lori replied quietly with a twisted sort of smile. "A ride in the country will be nice."

They filed through the reception office, Delsoto leading, and with Carmen guarding them at the rear. As the procession emerged into the entrance hallway they were confronted by two men in black T-shirts, DEA in large white letters across the front, their weapons ready and aimed at the man in the rear.

"STOP WHERE YOU ARE!" one of them shouted. "D-E-A," the other said, identifying them and quickly moved past Delsoto, Mike and Lori, training their firearms on Carmen. "Carmen Rios," one of them said. "Hands where I can see them!"

Mike spun around to see Carmen raise his left arm and withdraw his empty right hand from his pocket, both hands now atop his head. Apparently these two agents knew who they were after, and showed little concern for the other three. Within seconds it seemed, Carmen was face to the wall, hands behind him with shiny handcuffs applied, and one of the agents was removing the gun and three cell phones from his pockets.

For those few moments, Mike, Lori and Juan Delsoto stood silent and motionless, mostly in shock with the sight of the swift actions of the D.E.A. officers. Finally, Delsoto took an enormous breath and let out a great sigh. Mike heard the familiar "You have the right to remain silent..." and he felt quite certain that neither he nor Delsoto would be the attorney Carmen would wish to speak with before questioning.

The two officers started leading Carmen toward the stairs, still paying little attention to the others. Their concentration was focused on their captive.

"Are we free to go?" Mike asked as the agents and Carmen began descending the stairway.

"Yes," was the reply.

"Can we have our cell phones back? He took them from us."

"Meet us downstairs at the door."

A few minutes later, when the officers had thoroughly searched Carmen Rios and secured him in their vehicle, one of the black shirted men returned to the sidewalk door where Mike, Lori and Delsoto stood watching and waiting.

"Sorry if we startled you back there," he said. "We didn't mean to get anyone else involved. We had followed Rios here, and were about to go in to apprehend him when you and the lady showed up."

Mike smiled and nodded. He wanted to tell the agent that Carmen was in the process of kidnapping them, but he thought that would only further delay his mission. Instead, he just asked if their cell phones could be returned to them. "He took them so we couldn't call the police."

The agent nodded. "Sure. I don't see a problem with that." He walked back to the squad car, and a few seconds later returned with the phones. Then he turned to Juan Delsoto. "Rios had a bank draft with your name on it."

"Yes," Delsoto said, hopeful that it, too, could be immediately returned.

"We'll have to hold that for the time being, Mr. Delsoto."

"But—"

"Sorry. Evidence," the officer said with stern conviction.

Had this arrest been made by Captain Vincennes and his department, Mike would perhaps not have had the freedom to be on his way. But this was the D.E.A. and they seemed to hold little interest in his involvement and the connection Carmen Rios had with the two murders. Although he felt this delay had used up valuable time, it was not completely a waste, for now he knew what had been at stake, and why there were several parties interested in the gemstones that tangled him into this web in the first place. Now he knew what had happened to the money from the sale of the DC-3.

Mike and Lori made their way to the rental car and drove off before the D.E.A. men had a change of mind. The drive to the Barbary residence took just under twenty minutes. Glancing at his watch, Mike was relieved to see that less time had been lost at Delsoto's than he had thought. A lot had happened in a short period, and his own uncertainty had made the incident at the lawyer's office seem like an eternity.

Actually, only an hour had passed since he left Crawford's place, maybe less.

On the ride there, he had talked very little, and Lori had wisely asked few questions. "You have an idea who killed Harlow, don't you?" she said.

"Yes," Mike replied. "It's more than just a hunch. I have some evidence of a sort... unfortunately not the kind of evidence that would stand up in court."

After that they rode in silence. Mike's enthusiasm slowly evaporated, but determination and a deep-down conviction that he was right kept pushing him on. He thought he knew the motive, and he was ready to bluff if he had to. If he failed, he could tell Vincennes all that he knew, and let the detectives take it from there.

A patchwork of late afternoon shadows and sunlight blanketed the Barbary house at the edge of the Pheasant Branch Conservancy. As he and Lori walked past the neatly lettered mailbox, he saw the garage standing open and empty, just as it had that morning. They ascended the steps to the porch and rang the doorbell. Almost at once he heard the sounds of someone moving inside. The door opened and Celeste Barbary stood there looking very classy in a pastel blue silky dress and high heels, a half-empty highball glass in her hand.

"Oh, hello, Mike," she said. "Hello, Miss... McKay, isn't it?"

Lori nodded.

"Please... come in, won't you?" She closed the door once they were inside, and then gestured with the glass toward a table. Beside a framed photograph of a smiling, posed Celeste, were several bottles of various liquors, glasses, and an ice bucket.

"Make yourself and Lori a drink... whatever you'd like."

Mike glanced at Lori and she shook her head. "No, thank you," he replied. "Not just yet." After a short pause he added, "Are you expecting your husband home soon?"

"Any minute now," Celeste answered. Her welcoming smile faded as she began to notice the somberness of their expressions. "Is... is something wrong?"

"Somebody shot Abe Crawford this afternoon," Mike said.

"Abe Crawford?" Her bright eyes were looking right at him and her brows bunched in a frown. "This afternoon?"

"Maybe an hour ago."

Celeste slumped and sank down in one corner of the sofa, reaching behind her to adjust the pillows. "Why?" she said. "Because he knew who killed Donovan?"

"It looks that way," Mike said. "He was in the apartment last night. I think he was searching it when Lori came." He glanced over to see Lori ease down on the edge of a chair. "I think he's the one who grabbed her, and that was only a few minutes before she heard the shots."

"Do you know this or are you guessing?"

"It's the only logical answer," Mike said. "Bridget Palmer still had a key to Donovan's apartment. She admitted that she gave it to Crawford."

"But why?"

"It's kind of a long story," Mike explained. "But the general idea is that Crawford was afraid Harlow was going to cheat him out of his share of the money for the plane they sold in South America. He knew Harlow was getting ready to run out, and I think he expected to open the safe and take whatever he could find that was valuable... diamonds maybe... as sort of a collateral until he got his share."

Celeste cocked her head as if listening to a distant noise, and then Mike heard the sound of a car approaching. He stepped to the window and saw the silver Mercedes roll past and into the garage. Another piece of the puzzle fell into place. He remembered that car. He had seen it only once, and had not thought about it since. He had not seen the license plate number at the time, so he could never prove it was the same car he had seen driving away from Harlow's apartment as he ran toward the entrance the night before. But it was the same make and color, and that was enough for right now to convince him that it was more than just coincidence.

Chapter 20

At 4:15 Fox Bishop watched the maroon Oldsmobile sedan cruise through the parking lot and come to rest next to the fence that surrounded the dumpsters. He knew the car belonged to Julio Martinez because of a recent registration check, and he recognized Julio when he got out of the car and walked to the front shop entrance around the corner.

There had been just moderate activity around the truck shop during the tedious wait. Three tractor-trailer rigs had entered the drive-through service facility, apparently for minor repairs, as none of them had remained in the shop for extended periods of time. Fox saw Julio moving about near the garage doors from time to time, so he knew his subject was where he should be.

A white Toyota pickup truck drove slowly up to the shop bay entrance doors and stopped. A few seconds later, Julio appeared from inside the shop. He approached the driver's side of the pickup and stood there facing the open truck window for several minutes, apparently conversing with the occupant. Fox glanced at his watch; it was 6:07. He started the camera and pointed it toward the garage doors.

After a few more minutes, the white pickup backed away from the doors, proceeded to the dumpster area and pulled up behind Julio's Oldsmobile. The driver got out carrying a package that could have been a white paper bakery bag full of doughnuts. He stepped over to Julio's car, opened the rear passenger door, and placed the package on the seat. He then closed the door, returned to the pickup and got in.

Fox jotted down the license number and pressed a speed dial number on his cell phone to reach his contact at the

Motor Vehicle Department.

"Ted... run this plate number for me." He read off the number.

Within seconds, Ted replied with the vehicle registration information, but it didn't match; the plate was registered to a Ford Escort, and not to a Toyota.

Fox called one of his partners nearby. "Follow that white Toyota at a safe distance. Plates don't match the vehicle. I'll get the City or County to stop him to check out I.D.... maybe get an address, but not to detain him. Stay with it until a squad car makes the stop so we don't lose him."

The Toyota truck turned southbound on Highway 51, which meant it was heading back into Madison. Fox quickly pressed another speed dial number to reach his contact at the Madison Police Department.

"There's a white Toyota pickup truck headed south on 51," Fox explained. "It should be passing the airport about now. Do you have a car in that area that could make a routine traffic stop?"

"Sure, Fox... a couple of them."

"My guys are doggin' him now. They'll keep track of him 'til your car spots him. Oh... and he could be armed, so use some caution."

"What do you want with this guy? Want us to hold him for you?"

"No. In fact I don't want you to detain him any longer than absolutely necessary. All I want is an address. The plates on the truck don't match the vehicle. I just want to know where the driver lives."

"Okay, Fox. I'll see what I can get done for you. There'll be two squads waiting for him in about a minute."

"Thanks, Jack. I'll owe you dinner."

When Fox heard that the Toyota had been intercepted by a Madison Police cruiser, he could then turn his full attention to the surveillance that was most crucial to his success. Nothing more had happened around the maroon Oldsmobile, but it was nearly six-thirty, the designated time for Tony to make his appearance. The camera was rolling.

And at precisely 6:30 Tony's navy blue T'Bird coupe rolled up to the dumpster next to Julio's car. The motor stopped and the driver's door opened. Dressed in faded blue jeans, light tan wind breaker, and wrap-around sunglasses, tall and lanky Tony glanced around the area, and leaned against the front fender of his car.

Fox was beginning to get a little nervous when Julio had not appeared after about five minutes. Tony appeared uneasy, too, as he paced back and forth along the length of the Thunderbird.

With the tension mounting, Fox did not anticipate the next obstacle. At the absolutely worst time, a truck drove up between Fox and Tony... and stopped. The 53-foot-long trailer completely blocked Fox's view of Tony, his car, Julio's car, and the entire area around the dumpsters and the garage doors. If the transaction took place now, Fox would not witness it, nor would the camera record it, greatly reducing the success of the mission.

Chapter 21

Orlando Barbary's surprised glance as he entered the front door seemed a bit agitated when he saw who was waiting. Mike thought he looked too refreshed to have been wearing the tailored gray suit and precisely fashioned tie all day. His graying hair was neatly in place and beneath the mustache a half-hearted smile came to his lips. He looked at his wife. "I see we have company," he said politely. "Did you offer them a drink, my dear?"

"Certainly... but they didn't want any."

"Won't you reconsider?" Mr. Barbary asked, but when Mike and Lori murmured their "no thank you" he selected a glass, added ice, bourbon, and a splash of soda.

"They just told me," Celeste said, "that somebody shot Abe Crawford this afternoon."

"What?" He put his drink down. "You mean... he's dead?"

"Mr. Barnes thinks he knew who killed Donovan," she replied.

Orlando Barbary swallowed some of his drink and sat down on the opposite end of the sofa. "And what's this about the sale of some plane in South America?" he asked, turning to Mike.

No longer in any hurry, Mike told Barbary about Julio Martinez and Carmen Rios. He explained what he knew of their activities and of Vincennes' theory about Crawford's unexpected, early return from Columbia.

"You mean... Harlow and Crawford transported guns and drugs, and then double-crossed the dealers?"

"Something like that, yes."

"You mean, Crawford flew the plane to terrorists in South America, and sold the whole works?"

Mike nodded.

"And then this lawyer... Delsoto... had been paid in advance, and Harlow got killed before he could collect?"

"That's the way it looks."

Barbary took a long look at his wife. "I can believe it," he said. "That sort of thing sounds like something Harlow would do." He continued looking at Celeste, as if challenging her to disagree. When she didn't comment, he turned back to Mike. "Do you think these dealers... Martinez and Rios... are involved in the murders?"

"No, I don't think so."

"And yet you say somebody shot Crawford this afternoon. For what other reason?"

"I told you why I think he was killed."

"Because he knew who killed Donovan. Are the police aware of this?"

"They are now."

"But you haven't talked to them yet?"

"No."

Barbary put his glass down as a frown formed on his brow. Mike saw the stiffness grow in his face, and then spread through his entire body. When he finally looked up at Mike again, his stare seemed desperate. "What I don't understand," he said, "is why you came here with this."

Aware that it was time to get down to business, Mike looked Barbary in the eyes. "Because, I think you paid off Crawford."

"Well, that's crazy. Why—"

"And you lied to Detective Vincennes when you said your wife arrived here at ten minutes after nine."

"But she did."

"How could you know that? You weren't here. According

to her, you didn't get here until five minutes after she did."

"Well, since she was already here with a drink in her hand, I think I was safe to assume that she was home by ten after nine."

"You told Vincennes that you'd been home all evening."

Barbary just shrugged, but he didn't offer any explanation.

"How did you get home?" Mike asked.

"A taxi brought me from the country club."

"Are you sure that taxi wasn't following your wife around all evening?"

Barbary's muscles tensed. "Now wait just a minute— "

"Okay, skip that part," Mike said. He couldn't prove that. "But you still say you didn't pay off Crawford today?"

"Certainly not."

"Then why did you withdraw ten grand in cash from the bank?"

The question caught Barbary off guard. He had just picked up his drink and stopped halfway to his mouth. He paused for a long moment, as if frozen in the sudden amazement. He lowered the glass and swallowed the lump in his throat. "What?"

"Ten thousand," Mike repeated. "Five from a checking account, and another five from savings... first thing this morning." Mike glanced at Mrs. Barbary. "Your wife said you were afraid she'd clean out your joint account. Instead, you did the withdrawing. Never mind how I know," he added. "It can be proved. You received it in hundred-dollar bills."

Now Mike was feeling a renewed confidence, and quiet excitement was building inside him, like a shot of adrenaline had boosted his enthusiasm.

"Crawford knew who killed Donovan Harlow," he went

on, sorting the facts as he spoke, and supplementing them with sound guesses. "He intended to collect from the highest bidder. Maybe if he'd gotten his share of the plane they sold, he wouldn't have tried extortion. He might even have told the police the truth. I didn't know him very well, so I can't be absolutely sure of that. But the point is, he did try to collect. He confronted you, and you drew the money out of the bank to buy his silence."

"That's a lie," Barbary protested.

"No, Major," Mike said. "You know it's not a lie."

"If you can prove it, why didn't you go to the police?"

"I'm sure Detective Vincennes will probably ask that same question. My only answer is that time was running out and I couldn't risk getting involved in the investigation at Crawford's place. Whoever killed Crawford had two things to get rid of: the gun and the money."

"Money?" Barbary said, sounding a little bewildered.

"Your money." Mike noticed Barbary's blank stare, but he continued. "A man who decides he must kill another man might promise money, and then set up a meeting where he could do the job. But he certainly wouldn't bother to withdraw the cash from a bank. But you did. And I'll tell you why."

Celeste Barbary had been sitting quietly poised with her arms folded, holding an empty glass. She abruptly stood, stepped in front of Mike to the table and calmly made herself another drink. When she had done that she returned to the sofa, adjusted the cushion, and sat down. She stared at Mike. "I'm sorry. What was it you were saying?"

Mike gazed at her with mounting wonderment, and it took him a moment to gather his thoughts. The tension was growing inside him.

"Bridget Palmer came to see me this morning... testing the waters," Mike continued to address Barbary. "I'm quite sure that Crawford sent her. But I guess he figured I wasn't worth bothering with after he'd called here."

"What are you getting at?"

"Crawford must've made the mistake of calling here early... before you went to work, and you overheard enough to learn the score and—"

"Now see here, young man!" Barbary glared at Mike, but Mike ignored the interruption.

"I think you may have already suspected your wife. What you heard this morning when Crawford called convinced you that she killed Harlow, and because you were afraid she'd do the same to Crawford, you got to him first, paid him off and tried to get him to leave town."

"Now wait a minute," Barbary said. "You're forgetting one thing here, aren't you? Celeste was in love with Harlow, or at least she thought she was. She was gonna run away with him next week. She wanted to marry him. She told me so."

"That's what *she* thought."

"What?"

"She told me that Harlow had the reservations," Mike said, trying to control his excitement and keep his tone calm. "But Vincennes said the airline told him Harlow had only one reservation... only one ticket... they found it on him. He was leaving *tomorrow, Friday, not next week*. He wasn't taking *anyone* with him, and somehow your wife learned the truth. He'd played around and had his fun with your wife, just like he'd done with Bridget Palmer. And now he had his chance to sneak out. Aside from gangland killing and professionals, I'd say your wife's motive stands near the top of the list. Or haven't you heard the old saying about the fury of a woman

170

scorned?"

He broke off his narrative with Mr. Barbary and abruptly turned his attention to the wife. "How long had you been here when we came?"

"Not long... a few minutes," Celeste replied.

"Where had you been?"

"Shopping."

"You came home in a taxi?"

"Certainly."

"You bought some things?"

"As a matter of fact, I did. I've always wanted a set of *Liz Clairborne* luggage. It's to be delivered." She looked at her husband with a bit of defiance in her eyes. "I also went to a travel agent... and... made a reservation to Nassau."

With that, Mike stepped quickly to the table and reached for the brown leather handbag, moved by an impulse of hope and logic. As he picked it up, Celeste started to rise from the sofa, but then realized she was too late and sank back down. When Mike yanked the zipper open, he got the break he had hoped for.

The money was still there – a thick packet of hundred-dollar bills. There seemed no need to count it. He stood there a moment, shocked, not only by what this woman had done to Crawford, but also by what she had done afterward. Shopping. A set of expensive luggage. An airline reservation to the Bahamas.

As the irony of the situation struck him, still holding the bulging envelope in his hand, Mike turned to Mr. Barbary.

Barbary made no argument. The thought of all this had crumpled him, leaving him at that moment a crushed and defeated man. He reached for a chair and lowered himself into it. "Celeste!" he said, sounding as if he had just been tortured. "Why? Why did you take the money?"

His wife took one last sip from her glass, leaned to the side and set the glass on the end table. Then she seemed to give the question some consideration. Mike no longer had any doubt as to her true character, for now her callousness was in full view.

She looked at her husband for a moment before she spoke. "To get away from this miserable place... and to get away from you."

Mike turned away because he didn't want to see the anguish on Mr. Barbary's face. He put the packet of money on the table, and it was then that he took notice of the autographed photo. The inscription said: *All my love*, and below that in larger script was Celeste's signature. But... something didn't look quite right. His heart quickened as he leaned closer to make sure. The signature wasn't Celeste, but *Cellie.*

"Cellie," he said quietly, several times. In that moment he understood why someone had tried to kill Lori in her hotel room, and why a second attempt may have been successful had he not gone with her to Crawford's apartment.

"Cellie," he said again, aloud this time. "Is that what you used to call her, Major? Some special term of endearment? Was it your nickname for her?" When Barbary didn't reply, Mike said, "I guess Donovan Harlow must've used it, too."

He looked directly at Lori. Until now she had been sitting quietly, the color gone from her cheeks, and a little fear in her green eyes. "Remember what you heard last night?" he said. "Just before the shots?"

Lori nodded. Her lips formed the word "yes" but no sound came.

"A man's voice," Mike recalled her statement. "You

172

thought he said 'Don't be silly,' but that wasn't quite right, was it? Think now. You supplied the word 'be' in that phrase, didn't you? It would be a perfectly natural assumption. But what you really heard was—"

"Yes," Lori cut him off, and now her eyes were wide and bright. *"Don't! Don't silly!* That was it. And then the shots."

"Not silly," Mike said, "but *Cellie.*"

"Celeste!" Mr. Barbary's exclamation sounded urgent, and it caused Mike to turn toward Mrs. Barbary. That was when he saw the gun. He knew then that it must have been hidden beneath the sofa cushions, and that Celeste Barbary had chosen her place there with care.

Chapter 22

After what had seemed to Fox Bishop an eternity, but in actuality only a minute or two, the truck blocking his view released its brakes and slowly rolled away. When it was gone, Fox was doubly grateful, as there stood Julio Martinez with Tony. He was certain that Tony had, perhaps, stalled a little, knowing that the unexpected truck was hindering the operation. As if there had been a commercial break in a television movie, Tony resumed the action with Julio.

It appeared as though Julio was insistent on seeing the money. Tony reached cautiously inside his wind breaker and slowly pulled out a thick, brown envelope containing the cash. But Julio also seemed reluctant to accept it. Without touching the envelope, he directed Tony with a hand gesture to go to the Oldsmobile, and instructed him to place the envelope on the floor of the car, where it was out of sight, and to take the white paper bag containing the *merchandise* from the seat. He was then to leave immediately.

Tony turned to proceed to the maroon car while Julio remained where he was and observed. With slow, deliberate moves, Tony went through the motions as directed. After opening the rear passenger door, he carefully put the envelope on the floor, retrieved the white bag, tucked it under his arm, closed the Oldsmobile door, and walked calmly back to his T-Bird.

Every second, every move, from the instructions given by Julio Martinez to Tony's blue car making an exit, was all captured by the digital video camera, and witnessed by no less than three D.E.A. officers.

As soon as Tony was well away from the truck stop

parking lot, Fox phoned another agent. "Tony has the goods. He's heading your way."

Test would be performed to make certain the cocaine Tony had picked up was genuine. There would be no merit in an arrest for the sale of two pounds of powdered sugar. So now it was a matter of waiting for the test results, and then finding the right opportunity to put a collar on Julio Martinez.

Fox punched the speed dial number for Jack at the Madison P.D.

"This is Jack."

"Jack... Fox here. Anything on my guy in the Toyota yet?"

"Yeah. The driver claimed he had just traded vehicles and hadn't completed the transfer and registration. But I got a name and address for you."

"Okay... shoot."

"Ricardo Garza, 935 South Gammon Road."

Fox was surprised that the white Toyota wasn't registered to Carmen Rios. "Okay, Jack. Thanks. Now I owe you two dinners."

Fox hung up and immediately pressed the number for his main office in Milwaukee. They were expecting his call. "Got an address for a search warrant... 935 South Gammon Road in Madison. Take the place apart if you have to."

He knew it would only be a matter of a few hours; if necessary, a magistrate would be rousted out of bed to issue the search warrant, and by morning, Carmen Rios would have a lot of company at the Dane County Jail.

A short while later, Fox answered his vibrating cell phone, expecting that it was the information from the test results coming back to him. Instead, he recognized the voice of Mark Schaffer, one of his roaming surveillance partners. "Julio is getting ready to leave," Mark said. "Looks like he's loading up tools and equipment in the shop truck... probably going to work on a breakdown somewhere."

"Or it could be camouflage for a rendezvous," Fox replied. "I can see from here if he takes the envelope Tony left in his car. We'd better be ready to follow him if he does."

All three agents waited eagerly for Julio to either go to his car before getting in the shop truck, or to leave without the envelope. Their tension elevated, as they all knew they were very close to making this bust, and they didn't want their key player of a two-year probe to slip away at the last moment. If Julio took the money with him, they were prepared for an encounter with more than one person at the rendezvous site. Fox preferred everything to remain here, at the truck stop, because he had become familiar with the layout, and he had optional plans in mind to execute a safe apprehension without endangering innocent bystanders.

At first, it appeared that Julio was headed to his Oldsmobile after he had the service truck prepared for the road call. He stepped around the corner, stopped and peered at his car for a few moments, and then, as if he'd had second thoughts, returned to the shop office door and went inside. No more than a minute had elapsed when he emerged carrying a clipboard, got into the service truck and drove away.

"He didn't get the money," Fox said into his cell phone. "As long as he's in the shop's truck, we can be sure he's coming back. But one of you, follow him... keep an eye on him, just in case."

Only minutes after Julio had left the parking lot with a D.E.A. officer following at a safe distance, Fox received the all-important call he had been expecting.

"Fox."

"This is Jim. Test is positive. It's the real thing... some pretty heavy-duty stuff."

"Okay, Jim. Martinez is off the premises right now with the shop's service truck. Schaffer is doggin' him until he comes back."

"Good. We're working on getting that search warrant, too. Should have it yet tonight."

"Okay, thanks, Jim. Keep me posted."

An hour had passed when Julio returned. He parked the shop service truck near the garage bay doors, walked through the garage area and headed for the truck stop convenience store entrance. Just as he passed by Mitchell, the third D.E.A. officer, he answered his ringing cell phone, paused a short time, and conversed with the caller in Spanish. When he had disappeared into the store, Mitchell contacted Fox.

"I didn't catch the whole thing... it was in Spanish, but he told someone on the other end to get something out of his car."

"Okay," Fox replied. "The delivery boy is coming back to collect. We need to move quickly on Martinez."

Mitchell fell in pace quietly behind unsuspecting Julio as he exited the store sipping from a coffee cup. Fox and Mark Schaffer waited around the corner with drawn weapons. They had both slipped off their outer shirts exposing the *D.E.A.*-lettered black T-shirts so there was no mistaking their identity.

The element of surprise was so great that Julio Martinez had no time to calculate any act of defense. The coffee cup crashed to the floor as Fox and Schaffer seized his arms, spun him around face-first against a wall. Fox holstered his *Beretta* automatic, and applied handcuffs. Mitchell read the Miranda rights to Martinez while a waiting unmarked Dane County

Sheriff's squad made its way to the garage doors.

It had all happened quietly, just as Fox had hoped, in a confined area out of public view. Martinez had been apprehended and taken away without having any opportunity to warn his cohort. Now, with the scene appearing very normal, there was little chance that Ricardo Garza would suspect trouble when he returned to pick up the money.

Dusk cast its shadows across the parking lot as the white Toyota pickup came to a stop behind the maroon Oldsmobile. As Ricardo Garza leaned into the back seat of Julio's car to pick up the envelope containing nearly twenty thousand dollars, he did not notice the black Chevy Suburban or the black Ford Crown Vic block any chance of escape.

Within moments, Fox Bishop abruptly brought Ricardo Garza's freedom to an end.

Chapter 23

Mike's first impulse when he saw the gun was to step to one side in order to shield Lori, as it seemed she still may very well be the prime target. Then he took notice of the small, blue steel revolver, pointed right at him. It scared him mostly because he could not tell what was in the woman's mind. Her eyes were hate-filled and possessed by something that no longer seemed quite sane.

"Celeste!" Mr. Barbary spoke sternly in a commanding tone. "Put that gun down! Put it down. Do you hear me?"

He took a step toward her, and then stopped abruptly when she turned the muzzle on him.

"Shut up, Orlando," she said angrily, and then satisfied that he no longer threatened her, she looked back at Mike. "And what else do you know?"

New tension began to build. He wasn't particular about what he said; he just wanted to keep her mind off the gun. Struggling, he took his eyes off the gun and looked up at Celeste, desperately trying to keep his voice steady and not show his fear. "Vincennes took your statements at the police station before I got there. That's when you must've learned what Lori heard Harlow yell at you before you pulled the trigger. And somehow during the time when you were all there, you had a chance to take Lori's room key from her purse. When she stayed behind waiting for me, you had plenty of time to get the gun... from wherever you hid it... and were at her room ready and waiting when we came in."

He turned to Mr. Barbary. "You must've known she went out, Major."

"I was in bed," Barbary said, "and I thought she was, too. When I heard the car start and drive away, I knew it was too late to stop her then. And when she came back, she refused to talk to me at all."

Mike spoke to Celeste again. "You were afraid Lori would remember what Harlow really said before you shot him. You were afraid Vincennes might find out what your nickname was and put two and two together. This afternoon you went to Crawford's with the gun and forced him to phone Lori. If she had come alone..."

He couldn't finish the sentence. The thought of what might have happened made him sick. He watched the mouth twist on Celeste's chalky face. She nodded, and her eyes still scared him.

"Yes," she said. "I didn't know Orlando had paid Crawford when I went there, but it made no difference. When he saw the gun he showed me the money. He said everything was okay, and that I had nothing to worry about.

"What he didn't mention, though, was that he, too, was a suspect. If the police had put enough pressure on him, he would have to talk. I couldn't trust him. He didn't have much integrity. He drank too much, and sooner or later he would have talked... to Bridget Palmer, or someone else. I could never be safe as long as he lived."

"You made him telephone Lori McKay," Mike said.

"Sure. By that time he was scared out of his wits. He did what I told him to do. But he didn't understand why I wanted her to come."

Mike studied her expression as she glanced to her husband, to Lori, and then back to him. He could tell her mind was at work, but he couldn't be sure what it was thinking until she spoke.

"Why did you think it was me in the first place?" she asked Mike.

"The front door was open," Mike replied.

"What?" She leaned forward, appearing a little confused. "I don't understand."

"At Harlow's apartment. You had dinner with him, right?"

"Yes."

"You drove him home. You said you left him on the sidewalk and drove off. If that were true he would have closed and locked the door behind him. His apartment door upstairs would have been locked the same way. But both were left open. That wasn't like Harlow. He locked his doors. If it had been a professional who planned murder, the killer would have made sure those doors were closed.

"And it seemed to me that if it had been your husband who fired the shots – and that was a possibility – he, too, strikes me as one who would be more thorough. He wouldn't run out in panic and leave open doors. We know Abe Crawford was there, but he left through a window into the alley. If it had been Espinosa, he could more easily have left the way he came in... by the office door. As for the two drug dealers, I think they would've been more careful. I saw them at work, and they seemed quite thorough. But the front door *was* open."

Then he abruptly changed the subject. "Whose gun is that?"

"Donovan's."

"You didn't have it when you went upstairs with him?"

"No."

"But you knew where it was and you used it. Then you ran in panic when you realized what you had done. Not thinking about it, you carried it with you, not concerned about closing doors. You just wanted to get away as quickly as you could."

Mike let out a deep breath. The tension was still with him. He could feel the stiffness grabbing his legs, and the perspiration trickling down the sides of his ribs. But he knew he had to keep talking. "When did you find out Harlow was leaving without you?"

"Celeste!" Once again Barbary's voice was sharp. He was aware that she had already said too much.

"Yesterday afternoon," Celeste went on, not even glancing at her husband. "I called the airline office… not because I distrusted him then, but because I just wanted to make sure the reservations had been made." Her voice dropped to a strained, agonized whisper. "They told me he had bought only one ticket."

She hesitated, and Mike could see a renewed rage flared into her eyes. "At dinner he told me there was some mistake, but somehow I knew. And Donovan wouldn't admit it until we were in his apartment."

"You went up to the apartment," Mike said. "The safe was open, then, wasn't it? What did Donovan do?"

"At first he couldn't understand why anyone would break it open. He hadn't been there all afternoon. He was like a wild man, and when I tried to talk to him, he turned on me."

Mike easily understood, now, as he recalled the impression she had made earlier, this volatile woman, who had the potential to strike back at anyone who did her wrong.

"I'd never seen him like that before," she went on. "He said he was sick of arguing with me, and then he said I was a fool… that I should know better. Then he admitted that he wasn't taking me with him, and he never intended to. He said if I didn't leave right then, he'd call Orlando to come and get me. I don't remember what happened then. I can't remember taking the gun from the drawer—"

"Celeste. Give me the gun," Barbary said as he began his move. With steadfast determination, his expression showed no fear now, and his voice had changed to that of persuasion. "Give me the gun," he repeated.

She shook her head. "No. I won't."

"Please don't argue with me. We can fight this thing if you do as I say. But first you must give me that gun."

Barbary took another deliberate step toward her as she leveled the revolver in his direction. Her lips were pressed tightly together, and the hand that gripped the gun was white with strain.

Mike was amazed and startled that Barbary did not realize she was not capable, at that moment, to absorb logic and reason, no matter how persuasively it was presented. But he admired Barbary's courage as he move ahead.

And this time Mike moved with him. He was not certain why, nor did he consider the odds. In the beginning his interest in the solution of Harlow's murder was strictly personal. When Lori had become a potential victim, his motivation was prodded by his fear for her safety. Now it seemed that his persistence had delivered him to a point of no return. Somehow he knew the woman would shoot again, and he could not stand by and watch it happen.

He heard Lori's desperate cry of disapproval. "No! Mike! No!"

Mike and the Major converged on the gun from different angles; that was the advantage. During that moment the muzzle wavered from one to the other. But Barbary was the closer threat. As he reached out, the gun discharged explosively in her hand, the deafening sound crashing around the room.

Before she could fire again, Barbary grabbed the revolver

and twisted it violently from Celeste's hand. With his free hand he cuffed her hard enough to knock her back onto the sofa. As she fell, her eyelids fluttered and her body went limp.

Mike let out a deep breath and his hands started to tremble as the reality of the situation hit him. He wiped his sweaty palms on his thighs.

Barbary glanced down at his forearm, where a small red stain had begun to discolor the fabric of his jacket, realizing, now, that he had been hit. He flexed his arm and clenched his fingers into a fist, declaring that the wound could not be too serious.

"I'll take the gun," Mike said. He moved forward extending his hand in an effort to assist Mr. Barbary, but then abruptly stopped in mid-motion when Barbary suddenly stepped back and pointed the revolver at him. Mike froze in another moment of total amazement, and watched the Major retreat another few steps to gain more space.

"Don't come any closer," he commanded. "This is the only evidence against her. Without it she'll have a chance." He straightened his shoulders and raised his chin. "I intend to get rid of it while I can."

Dumbfounded with such a statement, Mike thought he would give some legal advice in hopes that it would bring Barbary to his senses. "That will make you an accessory. You know that, don't you?"

"It's a chance I'll have to take."

Mike wanted to tell the man he was crazy, but then he started to understand his protest would be futile. On the sofa, Celeste began stirring, regaining consciousness. Her eyes were wide open, and it seemed the hate and hysteria had left them. It seemed, too, that she now realized what she had done, and the shock had drained all her energy.

But there was something else, too, that Mike noticed. She was watching her husband with an expression that he had not seen on her before. There seemed to be a curious gleam of admiration in her eyes, as though she was seeing her husband in a new light. When he saw the pain and misery in Barbary's gaze, he had a new understanding of the man, too.

Mike recalled the things Celeste had complained about earlier that morning. He understood that Barbary could be a little pompous, opinionated, and even demanding at times. But he had loved her, and he still loved her now, in spite of what she had done. To let him know that she finally understood this, she said in a voice he could barely hear, "It's all right, Orlando. Don't make it any worse for yourself. It's much too late."

Barbary gave her a quick glance and nodded, the only indication that he had heard her. He backed slowly to the door, reached behind him for the knob, opened the door and continued his exit. All the while Mike felt Lori's urgent grip on his arm, as if she were saying "Let him go. Don't interfere." His tension eased as the door closed.

There was a brief period of silence followed by the rush of footfalls on the porch, and then a struggle. Moments later the door opened again and Barbary was back, empty-handed and appearing quite defeated. Behind him followed two uniformed officers of the Madison Police Department, Detective Quinten Vincennes, and his partner, Arthur Reynolds.

Vincennes' observant eyes quickly assessed the situation. He nodded pleasantly to Mike Barnes and Lori McKay, and then briefly examined the revolver, suspending it by the trigger guard with a ball-point pen.

"Did Scott Newman tell you we were here?" Mike asked.

"No. He only told me about Abe Crawford."

"Then he didn't mention anything about Juan Delsoto, Harlow's lawyer?"

"No."

"Then you probably don't know that the D.E.A. picked up Carmen Rios."

"No. But that's good to know."

"So, how did you know where to find us?"

"We went straight to Eduardo Espinosa from Crawford's place." He turned and passed the revolver to Reynolds, standing by with a clear plastic bag in which to seal the weapon. "We found out that a restaurant employee had seen Crawford come through the alley last night. Unfortunately, we learned all this too late. And Espinosa was another one who lied to us. He did have a key to the connecting office door. He finally admitted going there while you went around to the front apartment entrance. But he insists that he only went as far as the apartment office. When he saw Harlow on the floor, he left at once, and forgot the menu he left on the desk. Lucky for Espinosa, he has a solid alibi for this afternoon. And when you weren't there at the Royal Palace, and I knew you weren't at your hotel because I already had an officer dispatched there to find you, I figured you must've come here. Of course," he added, "we were coming here anyway."

He considered the woman on the sofa. Her teary eyes still watched Mr. Barbary, but her limp body was incapable of escape. Vincennes nodded. "We'll see that your wife is well-cared for and that she is treated fairly," he said to Barbary. And to Mike he said, "Even last night I wondered if Harlow's death would not resolve itself as a crime of passion."

By then, two more uniformed officers, one of them female, had arrived to assist with Celeste Barbary. Two paramedics came in with first aid gear and were attending to Major Barbary's arm wound. The Barbary living room had become an arena of activity.

Lori still clung to Mike's arm. He covered her hand with his and squeezed it gently. "Come on," he said. "You should sit down." He guided her to a chair. "I'll get you something to drink."

"Just water would be fine."

He filled a glass with ice and water and handed it to Lori. She took a sip, smiled, and passed the glass back to Mike. "I'll share," she said. There was great warmth in her smiling eyes.

Mike sipped the water and tried to shut out the activity around them. Now that Harlow's murder had been solved, he wondered how soon he would be permitted to travel. But somehow, going back to New York didn't seem important now. One thing he was sure of, though. However and whenever Lori left Madison, he would be with her.

Scott Newman's report on the front page of the *State Journal* the next day informed the public:

90 POUNDS OF COCAINE
SEIZED IS LARGEST BUST
IN WISCONSIN HISTORY

Forty-one kilograms, or 90 pounds of cocaine was confiscated from a Madison residence in the early morning hours. With an estimated street value of $4 million, law enforcement officials say this is the biggest drug bust ever in Wisconsin.

Julio Martinez, Carmen Rios, and Ricardo Garza, all of Madison, were arrested and charged with conspiring to possess and distribute cocaine. If convicted, each could face life in prison.

The arrests resulted from a probe by the U.S. Drug Enforcement Agency, and also involved Dane County and State authorities.

According to a criminal complaint, the cocaine was found hidden in the attic of a town house at 935 S. Gammon Road, the residence of Rios and Garza. Investigators also found a scale, large amounts of cash, and other evidence of drug distribution at the residence while executing a search warrant.

James Bohn, special agent in charge of the Milwaukee office of the U.S. Drug Enforcement Agency, hinted that the three men may be a part of a much larger drug ring. "This investigation certainly is not over by any means."

ABOUT THE AUTHOR

Born into a farm family in the late 1940s, J.L. Fredrick lived his youth in rural Western Wisconsin, a modest but comfortable life not far from the Mississippi River. His father was a farmer, and his mother, an elementary school teacher. He attended a one-room country school for his first seven years of education.

Wisconsin has been home all his life, with exception of a few years in Minnesota and Florida. After college in La Crosse, Wisconsin and a stint with Uncle Sam during the Viet Nam era, the next few years were unsettled as he explored and experimented with life's options. He entered into the transportation industry in 1975.

Since 2001 he has six published novels to his credit, and one history volume, *Rivers, Roads, & Rails,* a non-fiction account of Midwestern history that focuses on the development of transportation during the pioneer days— steamboats, stagecoaches, and the beginnings of the Midwest's railroads—and the impact they had on the growth and prosperity of Midwest communities. He was a featured author during Grand Excursion 2004.

J.L. Fredrick currently resides at Madison, Wisconsin.

Made in the USA
Columbia, SC
12 September 2018